The
Colour *of*
Dried
Bones

The Colour *of* Dried Bones

by **Lesley Belleau**

Kegedonce Press
Cape Croker Reserve, R. R. 5
Wiarton ON Canada N0H 2T0

Editor: Amanda Greener
Managing Editor: Kateri Akiwenzie-Damm
Publishing Manager: Renee Abram
Cover Design: Chantal Lalonde, Poirier Communications
Text Design: Heidy Lawrance, **wemakebooks.ca**
Cover Image: Himiona Grace

Published by Kegedonce Press
Cape Croker Reserve, R. R. 5
Wiarton ON Canada N0H 2T0
Website: www.kegedonce.com

Library and Archives Canada Cataloguing in Publication
Short Stories.
ISBN 978-09784998-0-8
I. Title
    The colour of dried bones
Belleau, Lesley 19??
PS8553.E45698C65 2008   C813'.6   C2008-901201-1

Kegedonce Press gratefully acknowledges the support of:

Distributed by Lit-Distco
100 Armstrong Avenue
Georgetown, Ontario Canada L7G 5S4
Te: 1 800 591 6250   Fax 1 800 591 6251

Contents

Without the Sex

*T*hese days, free of tangled arms, legs, body parts, wet flesh making damp patterns on my white sheets in my white-walled, white-curtained room, trying to convince myself that I am stronger for it, I feel myself shrink. I have become a statue of sorts, sexless, hard, cold-breathed, fearsome in my wintry robe, and when approached I look with a stranger's eyes: elusive, saddened, punished from such denials. I take to sewing once again, reframing photos, making cupboards sparkle with my new energies, inventing new ways of passing hours without wandering back to his smooth stomach and the way it moves under new morning light, thighs that shadow sheets on moony nights, the hairs that edge down the side of oval calves, his quick tongue over mine, or those long hands that fall slower than syrup and ring quiet under the rush of dawn.

When I see Peter again, I lean on walls, swallow my coffee darkly, purposely shift my eyes downward and watch his feet shuffle back and forth beside the side door and long row of shoes. We're nervous now, edgy. We've lost the casualness of before, when we'd Eskimo kiss under the blankets or take naked pictures in the backyard at noon. I dart about, my hands fast. Blood thuds in my ears, and I notice that his hair looks different and he notices that I've lost weight. *I like how it looks sticking up and I don't cook much anymore.* The phone rings and I run. He exhales and I know his eyes are on my ass. No matter which way I stand, I feel like I'm trying to be seductive. I get through the conversation, aware that the bedroom is behind me, gaping open like a wide mouth. I see his eyes on the edge of the bed, trailing the whiteness with his green eyes, his body still, hard-lined, sharp-coloured. *It would only be sex. It wouldn't mean we'd have to cuddle afterwards or even eat dinner together. We could just do it, and he could leave, and we would continue our everyday things.* Peter's shoulders look stronger, his chest bigger, and his tongue moves slightly behind his bottom lip. I wish the TV were on, a car would pass on the street, someone would knock on the door. The silence is pushing me toward him, making me remember kissing the scar on his eyebrow, his tattoo-skin, the toffee flesh of his hipbone. His nervous feet kick the neat row of shoes.

"Sorry, sorry. Shit, I should go."

"It's okay, really. It's alright."

I walk around him, make sure not to brush an arm, a hand, an elbow. I try not to bend down too deeply, and the cool air brushes the small of my back where my jeans don't reach. I feel his shadow falling over my cheek. He reaches toward the door, afraid of my closeness, my quick breaths, jittered hands. I know that he'll leave, I know I won't protest. Without the sex we're just strangers, fumbling on doorknobs, and tripping on scattered shoes.

Oil Change

We pull into the garage, tired from shopping. My sister Billie sips at her latte beside me, wipes the frothy corner of her mouth, and reapplies her lipstick in the pull-down mirror above the windshield.

"I don't go anywhere without makeup," Billie tells me, sounding pleased.

"You know, I really haven't seen you bare-faced in years, come to think of it."

"I know. It's like second nature to me."

I glance at her out of the corner of my eye. Her makeup sits on her face fantastically. Swoopy eyeliner bowing over cat-coloured eyes, earthy tones splashed over brow bones, cheeks, lips. I don't think I'd recognize her without it anymore.

"It matches your hair," I tell her.

She nods. "Yes, that's important. I'll do your colours for you, if you want."

I don't answer, and instead watch an emerging shadow out of the window.

"Pop the hood!"

A dirty hand pounds on the hood of my minivan. I pop, he lifts. There is a gap between the green metal of the hood and the body of the vehicle. His blue mechanic suit shows through, crotch-level. I feel her looking at me. I look at Billie, smirking, pink-cheeked.

"It's been a while," she tells me wistfully.

"How long?"

"God, it feels like years."

"No way. You mean, you and Cal...?"

"Separate beds, almost six months."

We look ahead again at the same time, sit back, our eyes sliding under the curved line of the hood like two dirty old men. We try to make small talk, but fail. The young man bends over prodding at something under the hood. His tongue slithers out like a skinned eel and rubs against his teeth. From my position I can see the pink-nubbed, textured landscape clearly. His brows fall, his cheeks indented, exposing high cheekbones.

"European, maybe?" I look at her. She nods. *bonding*

"Must be, with that face. God he's young."

He pulls out the stick slowly, pale eyes dripping down it. Quickly he jabs it back in, pumps it several times, pulls it out, examines it with slow eyes. His face disappears and the blue material of his suit returns. I look at my sister. She sits trance-like, nostrils flared, hands clutching her coffee in a way that makes me look out my window fast, uncomfortable.

"Why don't you girls get out of the van? It'll still be about 10 minutes. Drink your coffee over there."

"Women!"

The young man looks up, confused. "P...pardon me?"

Billie gets out of the van, straight-backed, bold, and looks him in the eye. "Don't you know women when you see them, young man?"

Billie cheeky attitude

"I just meant..."

"Oh, I know what you meant..." She cackles airily and bends into him closely. "And I forgive you...this time."

"You do, do you?" He hurriedly turns his back and continues to line oil bottles beside the van.

Bella more tame

I get out, eyes down and walk to the pine-topped table. Screws sprawl scattered, silver heads glint under the fluorescent lights of the garage.

"Ohmigod, there's more of them."

She's right. There's one in the corner, wide-shouldered, thin-hipped. He turns and nods. I feel Billie remove her coat beside me. I glance at her and I can't help but notice that the top button of her shirt is straining against the pressure of her flesh under the thin material. Another one comes out of the bathroom, wiping his hands on his jeans, yawning, head back. He smiles at me and I feel caught, dirty. The first one positions himself under my van, thrusting the oil pan beneath it, grunting and twisting his torso under the heavy green body. His legs are long, and his shoes are too nice to be wearing to work. He should bring sneakers, just in case. His long body squeezes out from under the van. He turns as if in slow motion, sweat flying across the room, and looks at me accusingly. I feel lewd, as though he can read what I'm thinking.

"Miss, when's the last time you changed your oil?" Stern blue eyes under straight black lashes.

"God, it's been a while. I'm not sure, really. Last year sometime."

He saunters over, the oil pan held out. "Look. Hardly any oil. This is dangerous. Your engine will go. You have to keep check, every 3000 Ks. Don't let this happen again!"

I feel guilty for a moment. I nod, he turns and the bodies return to work. I glance around the garage, looking for the calendars featuring the naked boobs and half-lidded eyes. Instead, I see a crocheted yarn dog surrounded by a crooked brown frame. A mother's gift? A school project? I adjust my low-rise jeans, making them even lower. I feel the air brush my stomach from the open garage door, and I yawn back against the table when the Must-be-European looks over. His eyes pass me and I relax my body, disappointed. I feel Billie inhale beside me, the thrust of her bosom inching out. Her back is arched strangely, her backside pushed back against the table. She coughs to cover her laugh. I snort when I see her oversized breasts bounce nearly out of her blouse.

"Goodness," she sighs. "It sure is warm in here!"

We turn and preen to the men's backs, willing them to turn. The scrapes and scratches of garage work sound throughout the garage. What is wrong with these guys? The last garage I was at, I left pissed off from the lechery, the catcalls, the whistles. And now we don't get a glance when we need it. I watch the man shimmy out from the cavity under the van, nod to the other man who jumps in the vehicle and starts it up. One leg is on the cement floor, the other pumps the gas pedal, rhythmic. His head bobs to a song on the radio, he brushes his hair back with a black-stained hand, he picks at his teeth. Tearing my eyes away, I glance at my sister. She looks angelic, motherly, leaning on the table; soft, patient. I lean back, and the tip of a screw scrapes against the side of my palm. I don't yelp, just watch as a spot of blood appears in the middle of the scratch. Billie doesn't notice and my pain is sacrificed for the flowing, blue-backed movements that somehow seem synchronized with each other to torment us, tease us. I press my palm onto the side of my jeans, wanting to stop the flow, the streamy lines between my fingers, the heat. I suffer for the sake of the last few minutes in this garage, the last few bend-overs, floor spits, neck cracks, the final drags of cigarettes, the remaining back slaps and fuck yous, and quick glances and loud smirks and wet steps across the floor, and thank you misses for your business and please come agains and hood slams and door slams and slams and slams.

We back out of the garage, our hopes dashed, feeling tired, old. We get a high-cheeked curt nod good-bye, a slight wave and we pull onto the main road. I glance at my sister, quick. She is tapping her finger against the inside of the door—tap, tap, tap, tap. It reminds me of an annoying clock and makes me want to slap her hand. Someone in the car next to me is screaming at me behind the glass of his window because I cut him off. I give him the finger and speed off toward home, toward my empty bed, the crisp white sheets. I drive fast, deflated, the world whipping by beside me, remembering high school, first kisses and senseless summer flings.

Watching the Moon

*H*eady with anticipation, I run down the street to Tony's car. The door is already open, waiting for me. I climb in, and we head north, his hand crawling into mine. I see the St. Mary's River, and I wonder how I got here, so far from home. He looks at me, hot-eyed, angry.

"Did he say anything about me today?"

We arrow back to my boyfriend Peter again, like always. *Breathe deep and answer dull.*

"No. He just wondered why you didn't call me."

"But I did! Why do you hide me? Your dirty secret." His hand back on the wheel.

"Shut up. I can't stand the conflict! He's easier when I lie to him."

On edge, Tony judges me with his clenching jaw and pulls into an alleyway. There is dirt crusted around his nails, made shiny by the moon. This seems dangerous in the dark. I still don't know him that well. He doesn't care as his lips are in my hair, my neck, my belly, thighs. Where did I find him? I should go home where Peter waits for me, but I know I won't. Not with his breath in my ear.

"Don't lie to me. Do you still love him?"

"No, no, I don't." Not now, with his hands hot on my flesh. He burns.

This can't be real. You can't. Won't be for long. All I see is the top of his head, curve of his shoulder as he burrows into me. I push him away just to see how he will react. He buries his face deep in my belly, sighs and calls me difficult. I watch the moon for a long time, and can't tell if he is asleep or not. I enjoy this, the silence, the lack of effort. Finally he talks.

"Don't end this. Not yet."

"No, no, of course not. Not ever."

"Do you mean that?"

No, no, I don't. "Shhh...Don't talk. Not now."

Tony's hands, rough and coarse, clutch at my flesh, bruise it and his lips cover mine possessively. I can barely breathe under him as his long legs spread mine apart easily, hips pressing into me. I smell car oil, beer, peaches on his skin. I scratch him, bite his neck. I can tell that he thinks I'm scared. I'm not. I want to tear him off of me just to show him I have some control. Instead I push back, wriggling over him, lap at his heat. I pin him down, thinking how awed he must be at my strength. I like the way the moon covers his face and lights one side. Tony seems like two people to me and I don't mind that. I like it. I stroke his long hands and look into one of his longer eyes. He watches me lift my dress. No smile, no flinch, no look down. He takes and takes. I give and give.

"Don't feel bad, Bella."

"I don't. I really don't. That's not it."

"What is it then? Talk to me. Look at me."

"Shhh. Let's just drive. Drive. C'mon. I like how you look driving. Like a madman."

"Really?"

"Shhh..."

We drive toward Tim Hortons in silence, his hand tapping on my knee over and over. I watch his lips, the slow dimples that guard them, and I smile. I don't care if Peter finds out. We ended it, didn't we? I eye-trace Tony's neck, the red finger welts on his shoulder and watch him drive. I could do this again and again. He sees me and frowns. His voice is low, his nostrils twitch.

"Why don't we go on a real date? You know, dinner, something like that?"

"We will."

"We should go out for a drink tonight."

"No, let's just drink our coffees by the water. Please."

So we drink our coffees slowly, not talking much. The moon has slipped behind a cloud and Tony places his hand high on my leg. I am pulled toward him. The heat of his leg through his jeans sears my flesh, makes me sweat. The smoke from his cigarette makes my eyes sting. I should go home where it's safe.

"Take me home now. My coffee's done."

"Mine's not. C'mon. It's early."

"No, no. Really. Let's go. Drive."

All the way home he glances at me, accusingly. I know he is thinking of Peter; how I might leap into his arms when I get home, kiss him, let him have me. I try to avoid his eyes, but I'm bad at that. His lips sit tight and red on his face, his long eyes curled down. The music is static, the riverfront blurs blackly and the moon is an eye edging into my heart. I won't let him touch me, I want to tell him, but I don't. It won't matter. He always thinks the worst. I see the start of my street ahead.

"Just drop me here, okay?"

"Far enough so he won't see us, huh?"

"I had fun tonight. Call me, okay?"

"Tell him I say 'hi'. And, listen...I'll be thinking of you, Bella."

I slam the blue door and run fast all the way home, excuses flying through my head. I am hoping that the air whipping over me will wash Tony's smell away. I am a terrible liar, I think, stepping up to my front door. With a shaking hand I enter my dark kitchen. The TV is on in the living room. A preview for *The Wizard of Oz* is blasting in the darkened room and I see Peter's feet sticking over the couch. I clear my throat, nervous. My lips are dry, and my hands shake. I walk toward him with tentative steps. They echo loud on the hardwood floors.

"I'm back."

He is sprawled over the couch, asleep. His lips, half opened, gleam under the glare of the TV light. Half of his face is shielded by shadows. His stomach rises and falls slowly. He looks so peaceful and beautiful. Relaxing, I sit slowly on a chair and watch him, wanting to curl up beside his familiar bulk, but knowing I won't. My eyes trace the curves of his face over and over, until he blurs. One show ends on the TV and another one begins. I stand up, kiss his cheek and walk to bed.

Billie

I can tell that she still thinks she's beautiful. My sister's reflection in my round bathroom mirror is unflinching, stony under her close scrutiny. She does the same thing always. Tits out, lips pouty, eyes big, unblinking. After a minute or so of this pose, she'll turn her head from side to side, smile and then bat her eyes, pleased. She fluffs her hair, adds a dab of shine serum, licks her lips and appraises her neckline. Her boobs always stay big no matter how skinny she gets. She once told me that she'd bought the new air and gel bras to make them even bigger. She calls them her trademark, her babies, her curse. I watch her as I take my son's bath toys out of the tub. She's lost more weight. Beneath her short belly shirt, ribs are laddered down toward her low-rise stretch jeans. I suspect that she's stripping even though she tells me that she's bored with waitressing.

"Another day, another fucking dollar," Billie sighs, squeezing her boobs together with her bony hands.

"What time do you get off?" I ask.

"Any time." She looks at me and sighs, thinking I don't catch her meaning. "I dunno. Two, three. Unless someone knows of an after-hours party. Hope so. I'm wide awake, slept all fucking day again, then began to fight with Cal. I'm serious, sis, I forget what the god-damned sun looks like."

"Want some soup? Homemade. Chicken rice, too. Like mom used to make. I made it for the baby, but he hates it. I made too much."

"I gave up carbs."

"You're drinking a beer. Carbs!"

"I gave up *eating* carbs."

"Ahhh..."

I leave Billie in the bathroom, spoon myself a bowl of soup and watch my sister do her makeup while I eat. Her skin seems ashy under my harsh lights, her highlights too yellow, roots too black, heels too high. I stop the check marking in my head and wish that I had the nerve to sit down and talk to her, tell her to go back to school, go back home, go to church, go back to bed. Her back is arched and the crack of her ass shows above her jean-line. I can see her hip bone jutting out like a chin against the porcelain of the sink. Her boobs bounce with the motions of her mascara application.

"Fuck!"

"What, what?"

"Goddamn mascara in the eye!"

She writhes against the sink, pained. She looks pornographic and I'm glad I have no company. She twists and turns her torso, moaning in agony whispering, "Jesus! Jesus!" through her bared teeth. I lift my bowl to my mouth and drink out of it so I don't have to see her. The liquid is murky, oily, and the rice gathers like maggots at the bottom of the ceramic. I hate wasting food so I swallow it down, fast.

"Look at my eye! I look like a freak!"

Her left eye is red, teary eyeliner flows down a cheekbone, into a crimson-lined mouth. I look at her other eye, at the enlarged pupil, glazed, glassy. This is the longest she's looked at me in a long time, with the redness to hide behind like a patch. I can see the chapped skin under her nose, the tiny scales patted with loose powder, flaky and flattened down with thick foundation. I want to hug her, but I forget how to be comfortable around her. Billie's eyes catch mine, wring them out with their sudden steadiness, then waver, look down, away.

"They're not so bad, relax. It'll be dark in the bar, right?"

"Yeah, I guess so."

I leave the bathroom, wanting to talk to her, find

wanting to talk

out what's going on with her life, more about Cal, if she's read any good books lately, done any shopping, seen any good movies, anything, but the baby wakes up from his nap and I run to his room. He's sitting up, eyes closed in the semi-dark, mouth opened like a full moon, howling. I grab him, wrap him against my chest and bounce him gently. He screams in my ear, his soother tapping against my temple. His sweat heats my neck like the afterglow of a sacred fire, his hair edges into my nose. He smells like baby powder and milk and Bounce sheets and I hug him tighter wanting to keep him young, keep him needy. He quiets, hiccupping, and I walk to the kitchen. His head rests heavy on my shoulder, hot breaths beat into my neck.

"What time is it?" Billie asks, glancing at me.

"Five, a little after."

"Shit, already?"

My son hears her voice, lifts his head and stares. It's been over a month since she's come over even though we have different apartments in the same house. He hears her footsteps through the walls, the music, the laughter, and when I whisper, "Auntie," he'll sometimes put his ear to the wall and listen and knock and say, "Auntie, Auntie!" She looks over at me, twirls, her heels scraping my hardwood floors loudly. I don't want to ask her to take them off, don't want to say anything to offend her or she'll stay away longer next time. She takes a long swallow of beer, wipes her lip with my hand towel and asks how she looks.

"Great, really great." I look at my son, "Doesn't Auntie look nice, baby?"

He points a finger, amazed, "Auntie, Auntie!" He points at the wall dividing our apartments. "Auntie."

"Yes, it's Auntie."

Billie walks toward us, her hips swaying back and forth, slightly unsteady. She pulls out a chair, scratches it harshly against the floor and plops down on it. I sit down next to her, the baby leaning against me, his hot back spooned into my belly. My sister taps her chipped nails against the side of her beer and it blocks out my son's hiccuppy breaths. I watch her chew on the inside of her lip as she looks out the window. I want to ask her if she's heard me knocking, read my letters, got the baby's pictures in her mailbox, but I know the answers and I don't want to start her rage, her tears, her accusations. She clears her throat, jerks her head toward the baby. "So, how's he been?"

"He's on antibiotics again. His ears, you know."

She glances at him, he laughs. "Geez, he seems okay to me."

"Yeah, he's feeling better. He misses his daddy too."

"That son of a bitch, he's better off without him."

She gets up and begins to pace across my kitchen floor, her heels leaving black marks on the clean surface. She finishes her beer and slams it on the counter loudly. She doesn't want to go back to her apartment because she's fighting with her new live-in boyfriend, Cal. I've never met him, but I'm sure he's like the others. His voice is deep through the wall. I hear them laughing, fucking, arguing. When I pound on the wall they quiet and then start again once they think I've moved to the back end of the house or gone to bed.

"Cal is nice, really. You might like him. He's part Nish, too, so we have something in common."

"Ojibway?"

"Naw, he's Oneida, or something or other. I forget."

"Hmm...That's good. What does he do?" I bounce the baby, he coos, pointing at his auntie, eyes big.

"He's a designer. You know, clothes. You wouldn't believe it. My kitchen is a fucking fabric shop! No shit! Sewing machine on the counter, cloth thrown everywhere. He's good too. Made this." She motions to her tiny shirt, low-cut, hot pink, Lycra.

I look down and pat the baby's hair. "Wow."

My son wriggles off my lap and inches toward my sister, his lips mouthing, "Auntie, Auntie!" He stares at her four-inch heels in awe, little finger pointing, eyes rounded. "Look at him. He likes your boots."

Her eyes open wide, and she pats his head in appreciation. "Good taste, boy. Three hundred bucks. Max Azria. Suede. Dickhead bought them for me."

"Who?"

She jerks her head toward the wall, disgusted. "Cal. I'm pissed, for real. His ex is calling threatening me and he's not doing shit about it. I think he still has feelings for her. I'm fucking livid."

She continues pacing and my son moves closer toward her, smiling, whispering, "Auntie, Auntie!" He lifts his arms up. "Up. Up. Up, Auntie, up!"

"Do you think he still sees her?"

"Who? What are you talking about?" I'm busy watching my baby to make sure he doesn't get trampled.

"His ex! He wouldn't have the nerve to still see her, would he?"

The baby moves closer to his auntie, hands up, louder. "UP!"

"He wants up! Look at him, he wants up. Cute, huh? He missed you."

"I'll kill him. I will. I won't tolerate cheating. I won't."

My sister gives my son a cheeky squeeze, picks up her purse and pulls out her cigarettes. I know she's getting ready to leave. She brought no more beer and she needs a smoke. I look at her, feeling sick. I can feel a fury build, a desire to shake her, slap her, push her down and kick her. I wish I could scrub the makeup off her face, force her into sweats, order pizza, make her see how fun it is to play cars with my son, read to him, love him. I want to scream that he only has one auntie, that he needs her, wants her. She shuffles her feet, uncomfortable, and walks to the door. Her fingers fluff up her hair, and she looks at her reflection in the door glass, adjusts her breasts, eyes big. She looks like a scared deer on the side of a dark reservation highway. I don't want people out there to think that she is nothing but a whore and I want to grab her and drag her away from the night ahead of her. My son pulls on her pant leg, beginning to whimper and she turns the knob, wriggling out of his grasp. He starts to cry and I pick him up, shaking in anger at her blank eyes, her empty visit. I feel used, spit on, and I open the door for her wide.

"Another day, another dollar, as they say," she says, rolling her red eyes away from me.

I can't talk, my tongue is chalk, my lips leaden, my cheeks volcanic. She bounces away, the wind falling over her skinny arms, her sunken belly, swaying her away from us, fast. I close the door, double-lock it and I kiss my son's wet cheek. Hugging him in my arms, his hot breath on my neck, I see her picture on my living room wall. Tits out, eyes big, unblinking. I feel like smashing it, sending shards sailing through the wall, into her apartment, like arrows, pointing, accusing. My son wriggles from my arms, runs to the wall, puts his ear to the surface, whispering, "Auntie, Auntie!" I sit against the wall and watch him knock-knock until the tips of his knuckles are pink, until he gives up. Finally, we walk together over the black boot-marked floor, away from Auntie's wall.

Behind the Window

Peter waits outside at night, watches us through the window, as we slide over each other, silk-skinned, on the bed that he'd bought me. He tells me the next day that he pretended it was him again covering my body, winding my hair into his fist, knotting it around his knuckles, just like he used to. Nights I hear him in the garage, the basement, on the roof. Whenever I go out, down, up to check, he is gone. No trace. Just the footsteps and cigarette butts in a circle under a tree.

Tony and I have gotten used to throwing blankets over my white sheer curtains, to peeking out of windows, seeing shadows in blackened corners.

"Do you think he's out there?" Tony asks me, his caramel breath hot on my cheek.

"Oh, he's there. I can feel him."

"Feel this instead."

We curl into the low light of the hallway, his hand nudging mine into the corner, where he wedges me smooth against the wall. My back rubs on the scratchy wood, and I think of the flecks of wood flakes that flew up into the air when I refinished my dresser, and I cringe, raw-red, bleeding. I feel like a criminal with Peter outside and this makes me want to hate Tony, to hurt him, to stomp on him until he pleads with me. I can't though and so I crumple and let him fuck me in the dark corner. The wall scrapes my cheek as he lifts me, travelling over my ear, my temple like sandpaper up and down, back and forth. I can tell that he thinks my hand squeezing his shoulder means passion, that my vise-grip on his neck is ecstasy and that when I bite him I don't mean it, that I love it, that I want it. Under his sweat, I remember Peter's tongue, the thrust of his breath, the taste of his laugh, his windy mind. His deep Ojibway soul. I would forget who Tony was, but his hair is softer, his hold looser, his long eyes more potent against my cheek, less urgent, less hurried. When we're done I wrap his shirt around me, shrug his arms off of me and watch him.

"You like this, don't you?" I accuse.

"What, what?"

"With him outside. I can tell."

"Come on, please. Relax, hush. Let's take a bath."

Tony grabs at me, like always, and I feel as if he's in quicksand, yanking at me to wind my fingers into his, to pull me under with him. Without his steady need, his desperation, he would be beautiful and I would drop his shirt off of my shoulders, let him pull me into the bath, smile, but I can't be needed by him tonight. Not with Peter outside, in the rain, the cold. I want to sneak into my dark bedroom and watch him hiding through the window. See what he's wearing. Look for the little orange tip of his cigarette, the smoke. Feel his eyes. Let him watch me undress. If Tony wasn't here, I might let him in one more time. I look at Tony, guilty, and then get angry for feeling guilty.

"You go take a bath alone. I'm tired."

"No, no. Let's just watch TV instead."

"I'm going to make a bite to eat."

"Let me help."

"Go ahead. I'm going to check on the baby."

"What do you feel like?"

"Something sweet. With milk. Anything, really. Nothing that takes too long."

I watch Tony dart about the kitchen, naked, frantic, his long body elegant in the dim lights. Purple bruisy lines trace down his back, over the muscle of his shoulders, and they look out of place, like charcoal smudges on a blank canvas. The curve of his back is wet with dead sweat and the shadows play around his worried eyes, making him look like an old lady. He scrubs his hands frantically under the steamy water, knowing how much I hate germs. The motions of his handwashing makes the soft flesh between his legs bounce back and forth and I look away, not wanting to see.

"Put some clothes on! You want him to see you!"

"Honey, the windows are covered, remember?"

"He can peek underneath! Hurry up, put these on!" I throw him some long johns from the laundry pile and storm out toward the baby's room.

I am relaxed by my son's breaths. I pull the door closed, slide down the wall onto the prickly carpet. I breathe in and out, like they taught me to do in my karate classes, flex my fists hard and soft, hard and soft, over and over and over. I can hear Tony in the kitchen, shuffling cans, banging cupboards, his bare feet scurrying across the floor as quick as raccoons through a garbage can, and I close my eyes, fighting off the urge to run out and scream and scream and scream. I forget him and edge into Peter again. We sat here together once, he and I, the rectangled glow of the under-the-door light streaking our leg skin. We were listening to our baby breathe over the hum of the refrigerator on the other side of the door.

"It's nice sometimes, right?" Peter asked me.

"What is? Listening to the baby?" I asked him back.

"Well, yeah, but this, too. The dark."

"I hate it. I can't stop looking at the light under the door. Or else I feel blind."

"I can see you, every inch. I don't need the light. I can always feel you."

"Whatever."

"Really. I can feel your cheejauk, your chibowmun. My grandma used to tell me how man and woman need each other, how they can feel each other's soul-spirit, each other's aura."

"Really?"

"Yeah. I thought it was her usual Indian bullshit when I was young. So fucking stupid then, I was. Now I know that she was right. And now she's gone. Too late to thank her."

"I love you, Peter. You and your cheejauk and chib..chiboo..."

"Chibowmun. Aura. Yours feels beautiful, warm, soft..."

Now he is out there, in the shadows, somewhere behind the trees, beside the garage, in the garden. He comes back even after I threw him out. After our last fight. When he learned about Tony. He knows that we're in here, but he just wants to see. Needs some proof. He stays in the yard, blending with the fog, with the night, and I feel like he can see me, even though every window is covered thickly. He has been coming every night, he told me when he came to see the baby. Just to look. Just to remember. He watched me as he told me this, to see my reaction. I said that I would call the police. He'd be gone by the time they came, he promised. Besides, he knows I wouldn't have dared. The slow smirk, knowing eyes. Followed me. Reading to our son they followed me as I walked through the kitchen: down my back, legs, feet, up, up. Over and over. Twitchy jade eyes, still beautiful when angry. High cheekbones, sharp like corners. Thick shoulders beneath inky tattoos, pulsing neck, that rigid, fevered mouth. When I looked behind me, his back was turned, bent over a toy car, talking to our son with his silver voice. I was stripped, skinned by him, made breathless by his sharp recklessness, the fury. Now, inside the dark of my son's room I feel the same, with him out there. Tony knocks on the door, a quiet, timid knock.

"Honey?" he whispers. "Come on, let's eat."

"Yeah, okay."

I follow him back into the kitchen. The low lights seem bright and I notice that he's put on the long johns. They are too tight and too short. The table is cluttered with food. There are crackers, cheeses, dips, stale cupcakes, milk, coffee and small bowls of melty ice cream. Spoons and knives lay perfectly separated from each other, napkins are folded and fresh placemats line the table. Tony looks at me nervously, shrugs and motions for me to sit. I no longer want to hate him; in fact, I try to love him. I try to see the cuteness in his indecisiveness, the charm in his fluttery hands, sad eyes, in the eager spoonfuls that he offers to me even after I shake my head no. I want to appreciate it when he wipes the corner of my mouth with a napkin, lays his head on my shoulder, gently burps, licks my ear with a sugary tongue. I look at him and force a smile.

"Come on, let's watch TV."

"After you, honey."

I cringe at his words and move into the living room. I peek outside fast to see if I can see Peter, catch him smoking, catch him leaving. It is silent out there, dark, and the garden weeds lash back and forth under the rain. I see a cat run across the grass into the garage for refuge, paws barely touching the ground. I can't see in the shadows, but for some reason I know that he's gone home for the night, that he's given up. I follow the line of the garage roof with my eyes, down the side, across the fence, looking for clues, footsteps, hints of his shadow, but I find nothing. Tony comes behind me, pulling at me, yanking my hands, his breath quick.

"Come sit. Relax-time."

"Okay. Okay."

We sit on the couch, his arm draped over my shoulder, and he clicks and clicks and clicks on the remote. With each click I bite my lip, annoyed. His hands are long and smooth, his nails seem polished, too clean. There are no scars on his body, no twisty inky lines that edge out of sleeves, no tobacco stains on his fingers. Just soft clean skin, soapy, powdery. Open, watchful eyes. Jitter-eyed, flutter-handed. Sometimes he rubs aloe on the marks I leave on his body, worried, curious about my rage, my heat. But he never stops me, just looks at me with ready eyes, defensive, nervous. I reach out and stroke his shiny ear, sad for us. He turns to me, surprised, elated, and I regret it at once.

"What was that for?"

"Nothing, nothing."

"You want to...?"

"No, no, forget it. Sorry."

We settle into quiet, blanketed into the room, his long finger pressing the red button on the remote. Click. Click. Click. His head falls on my shoulder, soft, happy. Rough hairs poke into my neck skin, itching me, making me lean back against the couch and bite my lip so I don't scream and scream and scream. I quiet and close my eyes, tired. The TV makes me see blue-yellow light through my lids, and I think of rainstorms, windows and wet feet walking home.

Lipstick Marks

My sister Billie comes to me at 3 a.m. slightly drunk, red streaked, whispering hard so not to wake my baby. "He did it again." She breathes out, waiting for my I-told-you-so, and when it doesn't come, she steps inside and throws down her purse. Her hands are shaky, bulgy, full of red cuts and her feet are caked in mud.

"Shit, I'll take these off," Billie whispers, motioning to her shoes.

"Just kick them to the side. I'll move them in the morning."

They hit the wall with two limp thuds and she looks up my long staircase. "I'll just go up, okay? I'm exhausted."

I look at her hard, waiting. "Do you want me to call the police? Come on, what's he doing, just sitting there, waiting for you to come back? He's a sick bastard!"

"I know. No, don't call. I hate him. I do. I'm tired. So friggin' tired."

When she speaks a cut on her lip reopens and she sucks the blood out of it, hurried, neat. "I'll just get some joggers on and go to bed. Come on, please. We'll go out for breakfast at Jenny's in the morning. We'll bring the baby. Talk then."

Billie walks up the stairs with soft pads, one foot bare, one covered with a brown-bottomed wool sock. I see that she has gained weight again, let her hair grow long, and I realize that I haven't seen her since the summer, since I've moved. She lives six blocks away, with Cal. Upstairs in their yellow brick rental, curtains always drawn, buzzer always broken. The last time I stopped by, she called later when I got home.

"Sorry I didn't come down. He was there. You know how he feels about you."

"I don't care. I want to see you. I was bringing a cheesecake!"

"Oh. He was there. I didn't want you guys to fight."

"For fuck's sake, you're my sister. I have more right to see you than he does, the bastard! Mom's worried. You never call and the baby wants to see his aunt!"

"How is he?"

"Who?"

"The boy."

"He's good. Big. He misses you. He has no other family here. He wants to see you. It's been a long time. These late night calls just don't cut it. Shit!"

"I'll stop by in a few days. Cal's not working again, but I'll pop by anyway."

"Yeah, yeah."

Click. Click. I hated her for a minute then. To stay with him and to never come and see me. With his big fists and fat, smiley face. Glinty teeth, black eyes. When she met him, she said he was just a fling. It was her birthday. She was tanned, bikinied, beautiful.

"I'm not into so many tattoos, you know. He's got 'em everywhere!"

"*Every*where?" I asked her, joking, digging into my party dip.

"Almost...you know. He's not my type, but he's fun for now. Until I meet someone more like me. I'll just call him, you know, whenever..."

"What does he do?"

"Besides fuck like a prize horse? Nothing. He's between jobs right now. That's all he said. We didn't do much talking, really."

"But you were with him all night! Almost twelve hours!"

"Yeah..." she cackled merrily, leaning back, showing off her lined stomach, her white teeth shiny and smooth, long hands running through her hair.

That was over a year ago. I sigh and go put on some water for tea, knowing that my sleep is over. I hear her padding about upstairs, the water going on and off, her quiet sobbing, but I leave her be. I can't talk to her about him without my rage taking over. I want to pick up my bat, go over to her house and beat him, but know that would never happen. I look down at my pregnant belly, rub it, and feel the baby inside try to swat at my hand. We do this, play back and forth. I know it's a boy, and he knows I'm his mama. I sit hugely on one of my old-fashioned painter's chairs, the butterfly indent pressing into my back through my old lady nightie, and smile despite the situation. I can hear my two-year-old son breathe from the pullout couch where we fell asleep in the living room. Quick, snorty little puffs, like the choo-choo train sounds that I make to him when telling him a story. I hear the whistle blow on the kettle and I get up and turn it off. I choose chamomile and go sit down in the dark living room. I spend the rest of the night there on my leopard lounge and think myself back to sleep.

In the morning, Billie shakes me. "You look funny. Like a big, anchored boat."

I look at my sister, confused by her puffy, bruised face for a minute, and then, remembering, sit up and try to smile. "Gee thanks."

"I made us coffee. Have a cup with me before the baby gets up."

"Alright."

I stretch and watch her limp into the kitchen. From behind she looks like a different woman. Wider than I've ever seen her, slumpier, messier. When we were young we called her the Ojibway Miss America, because she would never go out without makeup, the perfect accessories, an even tan. Her nails would match her lipstick; her shoes, her purse, her jacket neatly connected. Now there are holes in her out-of-style jogging pants and her nails are all chewed off. She turns back and smiles and I am horrified. Her head is like a mushy pumpkin, and the baby leaps inside of me with my reaction. I feel dizzy, sick with rage and I promise myself that I will not let her leave this time. I am finally going to get this guy. She brings the coffee on a tray, reminiscent of her old waitressing days, and we sip slowly.

"Please don't go back to him. Stay with me for a while. We'll have fun."

"Yeah, of course." Billie smiles at me, angelic.

"Cal doesn't deserve a beautiful girl like you. He needs a punching bag instead."

"Let's not talk about him. Please. It makes my head pound."

I watch her pretend that the coffee on her lips doesn't hurt. "I thought I'd look worse than I look," she says. "Shit, I know I feel worse. I don't look so shabby."

I look down into my coffee cup, notice she put too much cream in and don't say anything. I can't tell her that I've never seen her look worse, or older, or softer. I can't tell her that she's not beautiful anymore, or sparkly, or happy. I want to, but I can't be honest like I used to.

"I could start a new life..." she sighs. "I'll find a place right around here, buy some new things. We can go shopping!" She looks excited. "It would be nice living alone again, redecorating. I'm going to go through all my stuff and throw out what I don't need, and just, you know, start over!"

"It wouldn't be that hard. We can hit all the thrift stores. Buy some material. Cover some pillows. You know. It'd be fun. Mom could come down and help. She'd be thrilled to come down and help."

She sits up straighter. "Yeah, she would be thrilled. I miss her. I miss her giggles. Her funny curly hair." She pauses. "I miss Dad too. It feels like he died so long ago when really it's only been five years."

"Because he was sick for so long. He wasn't really all there since we were little."

"Remember what he used to say?"

"What?"

"That no man begins to be until he has seen his vision."

"Yeah. It's true though."

"Well, when the fuck am I ever gonna see my vision? Any vision. Even a glimpse. I'm so confused. It would be nice to begin to understand how to be."

"Sure would, wouldn't it. It'll come. For both of us. When we seek it, maybe. Really, what have we been doing to deserve a frigging vision? Come on. Maybe we should go to a sweat together. Dad always said to go to a sweat when we need to heal."

"We should. We really should. It would be great. Together. Dad would be looking down from the great hunting ground, smiling at us." She paused, her voice catching. "Anyway, enough reminiscing. Let's relax and drink our java."

We laugh and finish our coffee, watching the shine of the sun through the window beside my twinkly Christmas lights, my Christmas tree made crooked from my son and my cats. She sighs and sounds teary, "God, it's so quiet here. So Christmassy. Want to go shopping later?"

"Yeah. We'll push the baby around, pick out some nice stuff. I've got a doctor's appointment at 10. After that we'll go. Do you want to come?"

"I'll stay here, sleep, shower, get ready, okay? I'll be all ready when you come back." She leans back on the lounge beside me and closes her eyes. I tiptoe away. When my son wakes, he can't look away from her. "Who dat? Who dat?" he whispers, clutching my leg.

"It's your auntie, silly!"

"Who dat? Mommy, who dat?"

"I told you. It's Auntie Billie!"

He backs away and watches her with big eyes until we leave for my appointment. All the way there and all the way back he smiles at me whispering, "Auntie at my house. Auntie at my house." When we return the door is unlocked, and the house is black. We look all over the house, under tables, behind shower curtains, but she is gone. My son double-checked, triple-checked, screaming, "Auntie! Auntie!" but she never comes out. All she has left are her mud prints by the door, some blood drops on a pillow and half an inch of coffee in her mug, the red lipstick marks smearing into my mind like a violent dream.

Ali, in the Rain

Cold Sunday. Night again, and the heat of the chicken korma makes my eyes sting. She adds more hot sauce with long brown fingers and talks, her voice thick like sorrow. I don't hear her words, I watch them through her sad hands, the swoop of her wrist an acrobat, dipping, dipping gracefully. She speaks of sickness, pain, death; the things that make the world hurt. Then love, the questions about love.

"It can't exist," she states flatly.

I know she is waiting for my denial, my refusal of her knowledge. But today I can't say it. Not here, under the glare of my kitchen light, behind the sounds of our children playing in the room beside us, their fathers' imprints stamped on our lives, dampening the day. I feel her eyes searching for mine, so I pick chicken off a bone, scrape the smoothness with a nail, examine the pinkness of the flesh. She is patient, so she continues, her voice a lullaby beside the rain at my window.

I feel sleepy as I eat, as I listen, as I fall into the rhythms inside of this room. Her hands, her voice, the rainy stucco. The sound of my slow chewing, the swallowing. Her fork scraping the plate, the delicate breaths between her words.

"In my country, they say to marry someone who loves you more than you love them." She nods, eyes downcast. "Then they will always work to make you happy." She pauses, laughing shortly. "I should have done this. But now, you know, it is too late."

I look at her, thinking she must be joking. She is not. She is 30, lovely, tired from her losses, too young for such regrets. Her eyes slide over our meal thoughtfully, breaking apart a thick piece of Nan, sesame seeds dropping onto the chipped wood of my table. They scatter soundlessly. I wonder about the importance of seeds, the greatness of beginnings. She sees me looking, and quickly wipes the seeds from the table, into her palm, holding them so tightly that her knuckles grow white. The contrast against the brown of her hand is startling, and for the first time since I met her, I can imagine her angry. I wonder how long she's held it in, this rage. Her hands, white and seething. I have to look away. I meet her eyes.

"Life will change," I tell her, not having the ability today to explain, like I always do. Instead I sigh, look down, think about checking on the children. I hear a loud bang, giggling and a patter of steps. I change my mind.

We are full. She leans back, the turquoise of her sari pulled tight against her rib cage, her belly, the jewels straining forward, glinting under my kitchen lights. Dark hair over lidded eyes, she looks up, thoughtful, probing my eyes with sterile hope. We have had this conversation before, but not on rainy days, which changes everything. I can't explain this, so I don't try. How can I describe to her how the rain-prints on my window gleam like flesh-sweat down his back, the tap-tap of his heart under my chin, the grey air thick like his heat? She does not need this, just a quiet nod that we are better off here, stronger, sharper without them. And we are. Just not on cold Sundays. Not inside of the rains of spring.

"Do you want some more? I brought plenty." She motions to the feast on my table.

"I'm fine, just tired, tired." I smile. It is forced, pulls my cheeks apart painfully.

"Me too. It's getting late. Do you want me to go?"

"No, let's clean up and sit down, have a tea, watch the boys."

Her hands are quick, fingers long. I always find myself watching her hands—sometimes more than her face—when she talks. There are too many questions in her eyes, and in her hands are answers. Pink flesh between fingers, dry and chaffed, sorrowful. Tiny wrinkles spread evenly over the top; shallow, secretive graves, that scream to be opened, to be filled in, covered in warmth. Dry neglected pieces, patched like grass, unwatered, unloved. Graceful, diligent, they are the hands of a mother, moving when silent, busy while thinking. She never notices me watching, not even when she spreads thick-smelling hand cream over them, over and over, rolling over into each other like two lovers. They suck up the moisture and thirst for more, but she doesn't give it.

The tea brews quickly, howling for our attention.

"Let me." She is up before I can comment, clinking cups in the kitchen. She creates a tray out of a cookie sheet, lines it with a placemat and carries the tea and cups steaming toward me. She pours my tea humbly, and I remember her saying once that she grew up with servants in her home before she moved to this country. She sits across from me and we sip, the steam sweating our faces, and I watch her, wondering what she would look like inside of the colours of passion. I try to see her howling, naked, dripping with love, but I can't. Not when her back is so straight. Or her eyes downcast inside of her tea, as though the fragments of the tea herbs are speaking to her, her fingers clutched tightly around the hot cup. I can barely touch the handle of my cup, it is so hot. I am mystified as to how she tolerates the heat on her hands. She should be scorched, but she is not.

The boys tumble toward us, wrestling. My son is three, hers six, and they both like to wrestle, throw things, scream from the balcony until red.

"They get their wildness from their fathers. It is in their genes." She nods, dignified, her eyes catching mine. I look away, remembering Peter's quiet river-voice in the bush before the storms, how he would hide inside while I ran free.

I wonder about this, watching them, and think that my son is more like me. I feel like telling her that I love to scream, to throw things, to wrestle. Bodies squished together inside of rainstorms, limbs wrapped around each other, breath like lightning, thunder, thunder. But I know her mind is elsewhere tonight, away from here, thinking about the ends of things. My pulse is thunder in my neck. She looks at me, past me onto the pale arm of my couch, sad eyes covered with thick lashes. She could be a portrait now, shadowed by the nightfall behind her, outside of the orb of my lighted lamp. I smile at her true dignity, liking her more for it some-how, wishing I could deflate her sadness. She needs quiet reassurances today, everyday. "Don't worry," I tell her sometimes. "They're all like that. Losers. Momma's boys. We're better off. We're better. Off without them." And then she'll smile without her eyes. Those do not stop searching. Me. The tea. My words. Another life. But sometimes her hands will rest, perched on top of each other, folded funnily, like a pile of sticks, fingers stiff, stiff. Her wrist bones look sharpened, jagged, like exposed weapons outside of her pale shirt sleeves. I keep watch out of the corner of my eye, knowing I'm crazy, knowing her innocence.

She tells me things. Of fabrics, faiths, of giving gifts. Of convents, old friends, how bedroom doors were guarded at night. I learn her life from birth, taste her foods, hear the flow of her mother tongue, all inside of my walls. She fills my kitchen with spices, her hands mixing chicken biryani with my never-used wooden spoon, alive in her purpose, her mothering. I watch her wash and pray between the slices of occasional sunlight through my window. She seems so pure, sinless, with the light spreading purple over her eyelids, lips moving rapidly. I once gave her a baby blanket to wrap around her head. Even in this, she was noble. Repeated prayers. I learn of these, our early days. I watch her lips, the slow turn of her head. She tells me about a prayer that keeps bad spirits away and says she will pray over my son, as she does hers. She brings videos to show me the houses of Pakistan, the large rooms, and the dancing feet inside of them. The music of her movements. I listen. Learn. Watch her hands as she dances for me in my living room.

"When you push your hands forward like this," she explains, showing me, pushing outward with both hands, "It means that you are pushing the man away, that you don't want his love yet."

She continues, her jade sari twirling into blurs in front of me. She is animated, alive like I've never seen her, more beautiful. Head thrown back, mouth slightly open, hips twirling easily. I think that she does not know yet how much love is like dancing. I think of the songs of my reservation, the flow of feathers, the cool air over the heat of moving flesh. I think I might take her there one day. I mean to tell her, but I watch her dance instead, hearing drumbeats instead of flutes, smiling. My feet begin a tap-tap on my brown carpet, my father's own foot-beats in my mind.

"Do you like?" She shakes her hip between the rhythms. She is another woman from another life-time, and I wonder how she got here, so far from home. I nod and refocus, admiring the drip of sweat on her brow, the patch of life on her cheeks. She offers to teach me a dance and I think it would be fun to try. She peeks every few minutes to see that I'm still watching. I am.

This night she tells me why she loves the rain. Because of the heat of her country. Because when it rains her people make a breakfast dessert. Next time she will make it for me, or if we are tired, just pick some up somewhere. "Okay, okay," I say, the last of the tea inside my cup a puddle, muddy, too strong for me to finish. The boys are quiet now, worn out, staring at the TV blankly, leaning into each other between us. We don't talk for a while and watch Treehouse even as they fall asleep on our shoulders. Finally she speaks, just as my eyes blur.

"What is it like?"

"What?"

"Love. Not the kind with our children. You know." She pauses thoughtfully, her fingers getting caught in her skirt, "With a man."

The window-rain returns to my senses, sharpens itself into me and I am awake again. Inside of drumbeats and rainfalls and hands on the small of my back and wet legs inside of mine and teeth the colour of dried bones and heat driven by the thunder and thunder and the shock of reality inside of lightning and the spread of wildflowers on dewy grasses, pussy willows by a creek when he's inside of me, the lake grass taste of ecstasy, the spread of mud inside my palms and how his eyes look black when he's under me and scorched milkweed flesh and how he sleeps smiling afterwards and how we eat fry bread on drippy mornings after storms to keep our bodies warm, or the clashing of our furies or how pebbles cut into my feet when I chase him off of my land or how he tastes when he cries or when he's gone for good and the grey inside the sky and the hunger, the blur of weeks, the lurch of loss, the blank of quiet, the cold white sheets, the boxes, the rearranging of mind frames, the new faces without my son's eyes, the forgetting, the return to life, the comfort of a new man's hands, the power I dig out from inside myself, the new lines that fall around my eyes, the hesitations to fall into passion, the fresh indulgences, the mirrors with a newfound face, the thicker beauty under my eyes, the calm, the quieting of youth, the remembering of rainy days...

"It's nice," I tell her, gulping the putrid tea-bottom, fast.

"I'll bet it is," she says, her arms pulling her son into her tighter.

We sit together, the four of us, quieted by the long day, late hour and the spell of rain.

Tangled Hammock

*C*areless lives splashing by on this seaweed lake. That is why I am thinking of Peter again. The brown legs kicking out of the lake, sharp intakes of breaths, all of the squeals of youth and freedom cut into me, tarnish the perfection of my position inside of my tangled hammock. These things shouldn't bother me, these things should delight me. Summer air, butterflies edging around the trees, the feel of warm, powdered sand in my toes. But I'm annoyed, worried about wrinkling under the sun, thinking that someone can tell that I don't feel comfortable in my bikini anymore. I think about my children sleeping inside, worry that bugs will disturb their sleep, that they may have nightmares. He's probably drunk somewhere like this. Carefree with someone else. His son forgotten until he gets home and his mother makes him remember again. The stomach cramps return, the anger. One of the teenagers splashes another one and

I try not to look, try not to remember how it feels to laugh in the water in the summer, under the sun.

I can feel my legs pushing through the triangles of the hammock. I feel squished, stuffed into this thing, but yet I don't want to move, don't want to be anywhere else on earth at the moment. I remember beach parties, simple conversation, burnt hotdogs and Blue Light at dusk. Remember his hands with the rough finger pads on my back. Remember how his teeth glinted from the orange of the fire. I edge lower into the hammock, hating these young people with no worries, wondering why I chose to rent this cottage, so close to civilization. But my three-year-old likes it. Loves the squealy young voices, the appeal of colourful bathing suits.

My mother coughs inside, and Tony comes toward me, letting the door slam behind him. He kneels down beside me and I smile. Something in him makes me sad. Maybe the downward curve of his eye. Maybe his eager hands. Could be something else. His eyes seem to be opaque, misty. They are a cloudy blue, sharp against his cheekbones. Bronzed. Jumpy. He hands me a sandwich on a cracked white plate, and I notice that he used white bread, which he knows I hate. I don't say anything. Just take it and put it on my belly. I laugh on purpose and this shakes the sandwich.

"God, you look beautiful," Tony breathes. I always think that he's joking when he says things like this.

"Whatever..." I sigh back at him, peeling the crust off of the doughy looking sandwich. Some pinkish meat peeks out of the side, cold against my finger's edge.

"That bikini...I've never seen it before," he says, pulling on a side string, popping it open. "Hey, if I pull it like this, it just comes right off. I like this thing, babe."

He tries to pull slowly, but I swat him away, thinking he really doesn't think I'm beautiful. Angry at him for my thoughts.

"Are the boys still asleep?" I ask him, tying my strings back together, the sandwich falling into the grass. "Oh, shit."

"I'll get you another one. Your mom brought lots of ham."

"Nah, I'm trying out this diet again. Remember?" I pause, half serious, and glare at him. "I think you want me fat so no other man will look at me." I pretend to look away in anger.

"You have the best body in the world. Look at this. Look at this." He begins to grab again, and tickle, which annoys me, but I laugh, not wanting to seem uptight, not wanting to seem unaffectionate.

A young laugh from the water cuts through our own, slicing it apart, and I am quieted into my own thoughts. I look at Tony and ask him to give me 10 minutes to bask and then I'll come in and make a salad for supper. I'd rather him not notice the younger bodies and freer, lighter minds. Just something else to worry about. I need his admiration, his looks of love. Especially on a day like today.

"And then we'll play?" He pouts, making me want to shut my eyes against his puppy dog expression.

"Yes, yes, now go, go. I never get to do this. To lay down in the sun."

I watch his retreat and admire his long, muscled back, wet with sweat, tinged with sun. I think that he doesn't know how beautiful he is. Or tiring. He is gone with a loud bang of the screen door, which is followed by a drawn-out baby's howl. He always forgets to catch the door. I sigh, shifting positions, almost getting up to pick up my son. But I know that he'll do it for me and give me my 10 minutes. My breasts start to tingle, the milk rising, my nipples aching for release, but I ignore it, even as a round wetness spreads in two circles on the front of my orange bikini. The howling stops and I hear a tiny giggle. Amused, the baby will wait. I relax, press my hands on my breasts to quiet the flow and I close my eyes to the heat.

Spirally yellow circles dot the back of my eyelids. Lines where a tree branch was. Orbs of bubbles are sucked upward, make me feel dizzy. I open and shift, trying to turn on my side, feeling more tangled than ever. I know that Peter would like it here. At first. He'd

play with our son for a few minutes, then sneak off to
burn a joint behind a tree. Then walk it off so I won't
smell it, telling me about all the rocks he'd picked and
how nice the sun is, glinting behind the branches. He
would tell me that this kind of place is the place of
Indians. Can only be appreciated by the Indian soul,
and I would disagree, telling him that my mother
loves it here and she is White. And he would roll his
eyes and tell me that I just don't get it. And he would
get quiet. I would be able to tell that he'd be wondering if there's a bar nearby for "just a few", by the way
his eyes would trace the horizon, the paths, between
the trees for some escape. I would watch him as he'd
skip rocks and try to play with our son again until he
whined and then he'd ask me, "What is wrong with
him?" and I would tell him to try to ask him and then
he would think I was being sarcastic and then I would
hold it in because our son is listening and then he
would feel the tension and start to cry and he would
ask me, "For God's sake, why is he crying?" and finally
I would scream and tell him, "It's because of you,
because of you, because of you, because of you,
because of you, because of you!"

"It's time, Mummmy!" My three-year-old races out,
slamming the door, making me jump as he runs barefoot on the pebbled walk, not noticing the bumps.

"For what, sugar?"

"Salad time." He breathes, hot in my face, his breath always sweet.

"Oh. That." I look at him, the ruffled hair, speckled eyes, sandy eyebrows, tiny teeth. "Get over here, you munchkin, and sit with me up here!"

He crawls up, quick, and I try to regain the balance, but he is fast, he is eager, and wrapped in my arms we fall to the ground, my foot still tangled in the hammock. There is sand on my cheek, dirt on his chin. We see we're okay and we laugh. And I tickle. And we laugh. And he laughs. Tony stands holding the baby in his arms, watching my son and me on the ground and his smile is so wide and his eyes are so bright and the baby curls into him and my son's laughter vibrates on my ribs and I am happy and he puts his arm out and I take it.

Inside Your Sweetgrass Hands

Then follow me here if you feel lost. Follow me softly and I won't even know that you're here. Once, my grandmother told me that Indians aren't allowed in Heaven, but that she was sure that God would have a place rounded up for us that might be just as good. I didn't believe her, but I smile now at her voice, her serious eyes, her slow nod as she sewed a hole in a yellowed sock. When she died I looked in her coffin, touched her smooth, brown cheek and knew that God let her in through those gates that I heard about. He had to have. She was smiling so peaceful that I knew that she went in. Later, I prayed to God to tell my Gramma that I miss her and that I'll get in too one day. I lay back that night, thinking of the long line that must be outside of those pearly gates, and wondering if God will look at me or just skip to the next person.

I dreamed of God after my grandmother died, wondering who He is and why He let the White Man put the Indian kids in those schools. I wondered if He was trying to teach us something, or if the White guys were just practicing their freedom of choice and God will deal with them later, or if He was trying to toughen us up or prepare us for something. I would think of these things for hours, the hum of crickets outside my window singing to me.

Later, my father let missionaries in. They were Baptists, from the deep south, wearing suits, deep frowns and talking to my parents deep into the night. They came around and brought their children. Little boys and girls wearing culottes and knee socks. My sister and I agreed they looked like weird dolls with funny voices. But we played with them anyway, and soon we went to their rented house and my mother squeezed my sister and I into tight culottes and knee socks and I was uncomfortable and she sighed when I got a dead bug stain right on the knee before we left and when my sister's ponytail fell out and her nose started to run. We were quiet all the way there, wondering what the Baptists wanted from us, wondering why they just didn't go back down to the deep south so we could put our cut-off shorts on again and run around barefoot in the yard.

We ate green beans with almonds, perogies and cabbage rolls. My sister cried when she saw the puffy white dough, and I spit the sour cream onto the cloth napkin, choking. My mother gave me those eyes, watching me until I took another bite, forcing it down, trying not to cry. The culottes were too tight on my waist and my tummy started to ache. The knee socks were itchy and I wanted to go home. Later, they sat us down and told us about God and Hell, mostly talking to my mother because she was White and they probably figured she knew God better and she nodded and nodded and nodded and nodded. They told my father they wanted to help the people on the reserves and that is why they were here. When we left, I peeled my long knee socks off and stuffed them under the back of the driver's seat so I wouldn't have to wear them again.

I began to talk to God, asking Him questions. Wondered so much why He sent these people to help us. I began to see God as being big. Really big. With these huge hands that could crush us if we were bad. I watched over my shoulder, watched the sky. Shivered under my blankets in a storm. Always fearing those big hands that could pick me up and squash me flat. I started to feel guilty when the southern visitors looked at me. They made me feel like I was hiding something, like my clothes were dirty. Like I should brush my hair, pick out the dirt from my fingernails. I wondered for a minute if God got dirt under His nails from squashing people, but deep down I knew He didn't.

Years later, I was at church talking to someone out-side. I told her I was from the reserve and she said that she was glad I no longer practiced the ways. "Witch-craft," she whispered. More years, and more accusa-tions, until I stayed away, suspicious of the minds of the church, of the smooth white hands that patted mine. But still I spoke to Him, thinking of those big, hard hands, remembering Gramma's words.

Night falls and my sheets are damp from my sweat. Dreaming of faces and hands and words. Remem-bering drumbeats, the soft, slow voices of my people. The wisdom in those faces. The biblical words about wisdom. Night falls and my mind cannot sleep. Moon-light is bathing my thoughts, purifying them, hovering over the white of my sheets. It feels like thinking time, just me and the moon and our Creator listening to my thoughts. My back leans up against the wood lines of my wall, feeling cool, feeling natural, and I drift into thought with dream pulsing through. Somewhere here, between the slow think of the 3 a.m. mind and the rapid flow of dream, I see a big hand reach down, the lines through it huge, the mass of it mind boggling. But it is not here to squish me, it is here to pick me up. And so I let it. I don't crawl into it; instead, I fall back. It is not hard like I imagined. It is soft, scented. Sweet-grass aromas cover me, so much so that I look down.

The entire hand is light brown, vast like a field and I turn and press my face into it. It is made out of sweet-grass. Long, fields of scented flesh. I am not really sur-prised by this. I stop my thinking and turn to sleep, safe in your sweetgrass hands.

Somewhere, in dreamtime, the questions stop. I sleep.

Midnights

Tony sleeps. Midnight, and I am caught inside of it. A black orb that suckles at me like an infant. The children sleep, constant breaths that swoop in and out. I check on them, watch him, and try to wrestle myself into the arms of solitude. Today I saw blackbirds on the ledge of my balcony and took it as a sign. My mind blurs into legend and I think that it is an eagle that means something, or an owl, both? But not those black-beaked birds that stared at me behind the panes of my patio glass as though I were the intruder. I sigh and think to turn on a light, but I don't want to get up from the slow rock of my chair, not now, in the middle of my thoughts.

He did the dishes quickly and missed some spots. When I put them away, I noticed a small dot of ketchup on the rim of a blue-edged plate and it rose in me: fury. I scraped the plate raw with my nail until my finger throbbed and then put it away. I watched him

for the rest of the night, wondering who he is and why
he stays. They are not his children, but I think they are
starting to love him.

"Come here, Tony, throw me, let me come with
you. Pleease..." my three-year-old screeches, lost in
joy as he flies through the air.

I saw his daddy in court today. Twitchy eyes that
followed me, found me behind crowds, as I clutched
the new baby inside of the crowd. My lawyer saw me.

"You have no one to watch the child?"

"No, I told you..."

"Don't you have a sister?"

"She sleeps in, she is nervous around..."

"It's okay, we'll talk out here."

"I'm breast-feeding, it's hard to..."

"Let's discuss the restraining order. You have to
stop talking to him in court."

"I don't. I am answering him. He finds me, I mean,
look at him, he is..."

"Read this, and sign if you agree."

"Okay, okay..." I signed, my signature shaky from
the baby squirming under my new movements, Peter's
eyes on me from across the room, leaving drumbeats
in my neck pulse.

When I left, the heaviness in my chest was there
until I turned the corner, away from the stone grey
walls of the courthouse. I stroked the baby's cheek.

"I'm sorry, I'm sorry little one." He looked at me with startled eyes, round o's that pull at me, propel me toward home. I think that I would kill anyone who hurts him, wondering at the same time if my mother thought that of me.

Tony was already there when I got home, shoes scattered by the front door, bacon sizzling from the kitchen.

"BLTs honey. You hungry?"

I was, but I didn't want to give him the satisfaction of being right, as usual. "Not really. Court turns my stomach."

"How did it go? Did Peter talk to you again?" Concern. It is real, I know.

The smell of the bacon reached into me, my tongue swirls around my mouth, remembering. Water. He rubbed my shoulders. "Yeah, you know, the usual."

"I'm sorry, I'm sorry." Hovering, wanting me to touch him back.

"The bacon's burning. Hurry, hurry!"

He worked fast. Sandwiches piled up, bits of bacon, tomato, still-wet lettuce pieces. I grabbed and chewed, fast, fat swallows edging down my throat. It was salty, crisp, perfect. The baby woke and still I ate, wanting milk. Tony saw this in me, a glass appeared before me. I didn't thank him. Patted his hand and nodded. The thickness of bread on my palate, the plump of child against my arm, the smooth of milk cold in my chest. He saw then somehow that I needed him. I didn't want to need him when I let him in, so how did it happen? He saw, and I turned and walked away, slamming the bathroom door behind me.

Now it is midnight and I cannot leave the day. My mind is alive, buzzing with fire. I don't sleep much and this could account for the dizziness, days of forgetfulness, the long periods of staring. Things too loud, too bright, too fast.

"It's just postpartum depression," my sister told me. "Hell, try having it five times. Worse each time. This time, I tell you, I'm so used to it, I get nervous when I start to feel normal again."

She just had number five. An accident. An impossibility, her doctor said. A miracle, I suggested. "Naw, I'm just really fertile, that's all," she shrugged.

Our babies are two days apart. Mine first. She wanted them on the same day. "Hold on," she told me when I called to warn her that my labour began. "For God's sake, drag it out!" she screamed over the phone from Sault Ste. Marie. "We could have double parties! I still have two days left!" She has Cesareans. Not by choice, of course, she reminds me. "My pelvic wall is too narrow, is all."

Drag it out? I tried, I really did, but it didn't work. He came, red-faced, howling. I was struck with a long headache and the nurses made me lay back, and I could only hear him, see his blur while they did things to him. I was convinced that it was a complication from the epidural. "Don't take the epidural," my girl-friend warned me before I went in. "It will harm you in the long run! I have back problems. I was paralyzed on one side for two weeks. Please don't! Promise me!"

I promised until I felt the pain. Until yellow dots exploded behind my eyelids, until I heard a long, drawn-out scream erupt from my throat. Until I wanted to die. In my pain I wondered how my grand-mother had twelve babies in the bush on the reserve without a doctor, her sisters chanting around her qui-etly, wiping her brow, easing the baby out of her body. I wished that I had that now, the help from my sisters, the firelight, the freedom to scream it out in the bush, the sympathy from the animals around me, the night sky, the crackle of wood burning, the smell of dirt under my nose. Instead of the lights in my face, the strange voices, the women I never met before in nurse's uniforms, the unsmiling doctor with shiny glasses, the cold bed under my legs, the stark white walls, the silence. All I had of the earth I could not even see through the window that stared blackness back at me, unwilling to save me.

Later, giving up, I bent over, hunched, and took the thick coldness in my spine, happily. Felt the ice trickle into me, stretch down into my abdomen, legs. Relaxed into painlessness. Let the baby come quickly, without pain, without pain, without the pain. Watching the doctor's face, hearing the nurses' quick breaths, seeing my mother wring her hands beside me, her eyes wild. Slithered wetly from me under the spotlight, under the many watchful eyes. I wondered briefly who all these people were and then, just as quickly, did not care.

And now the night is slow in my sleepiness. The children sleep, and Tony sleeps, their breath constant swoops in and out, and I am jealous of their peacefulness, envious of their ability to fall so easily into rest. I rock back and forth, thinking on things, trying to calm the midnight questions, the ones that hide during the light of day, but I can't. It's not the coffee. I gave it up. I should be sleeping, curled into the corner of my bed, blankets sprawled around me, hugging my pillow like a happy lover, but I'm not. Here, the midnight noises whirr into my brain, edge me toward fear, the squeak of my rocking chair annoys me, the cars on the street remind me that there are people with places to go.

Tony sometimes snores, and tonight it is grating. Puffs of sharp breaths, nose-whistles that make me want to shake him, kick him in his sleep, watch him wake up in fear. Make him lose his sleep just because I am. I rise to the bedroom door to watch him. See his naked chest rise up and down, black curly hairs spread randomly in the middle of his flesh. His mouth is open, slack. Lips quiver with each exhalation. Today he bothers me more than ever and I vow to throw him out soon. I have threatened him before, but he has stopped believing me.

"This time I mean it!" I was in a rage, just threw the toaster, little brown crumbs covering the white linoleum. I worried briefly about ants, and then continued. "You think that I can't do this on my own, don't you? You want me to become dependent on you. You want me to need you, that's why you do all these things for me, for your own selfish motives. You are selfish! Selfish!"

"Your hormones are acting up. You don't mean it. Relax, honey, relax. Breathe," he crooned, giving me a sympathetic look.

I stomped out to the balcony that day, glad my son was at daycare. I felt the baby kick inside of me, thinking for a moment how his father is missing all of his moments and hating him for it, despise him again and again and again. Hate him for all his lies, hypocrisy. How he spoke of respecting the earth, the body, the family and then drank all night, forgetting us. I looked out at the parking lot and then behind me into the kitchen, watching the man who is not the father on his hands and knees hand sweeping the crumbs into the garbage. Tony never complained—not once—of all my rage. He never yelled back, never stopped me from hitting. Just waited until I'd stop and flop down on the couch, tired. And then he'd sit beside me and hold my hand and tell me things. "Everything is okay. You're such a good mother. It's his fault, not yours. You are beautiful. I love you. I love you."

And at midnights like these, I don't know what to do. With fathers. With long drawn-out days that fall into fogginess, leaving me emptied, sucked dry. With signing my name at the bottom of papers, forgetting to read what is on the top. With school work. With empty cupboards. With mechanics who say to get rid of it, that it's not worth it to try to fix again. With hot foreheads in the middle of the night. With screaming in-laws. With mothers who think that I am the strong one. With my sister's laundry. With Sundays. And with a soft-eyed man who maybe I could love.

Tiny Blueberries

*I*t's strange now to be here, back in the abandoned yard, waist deep in burnt ferns and smushed snake-berries. The old house is shadowed by the branchy tree limbs that hang above us like angry grandmothers. I am nervous and can't understand why. The garage is to my right, black siding half slid off, and the door unhinged, hanging like a corpse. Trees everywhere. Shadows crowding between them, turning the backdrop into grey. Throngs of bush-breaths to welcome me back to the reserve. It's been only five years and the damage, the overgrowth, is incredible. There are beer caps scattered. Flicked over the yard. One on top of my chihuahua's grave, her homemade wooden stick cross cast to the side of the garage, the name "Bambi" barely readable. I bend and pick it off. Put it in my pocket just to get it out of the yard.

My boyfriend, Tony, has never been here. Just heard of my bountiful Indian land where I will rebuild all of my dreams one day. His eyes are uncertain to its beauty, stunned at the weeds, the branches everywhere. His feet walk as though expecting snakes or wolves to lunge out from behind the debris. I tread forward, suddenly angry at the wreckage, the careless acres of shunned wonder.

"Let's go in," I tell him, motioning to the house.

Tony pulls a crumpled pack of DKs out of his pocket, pulls out a smoke and lights it. "I'll be right there, babe. Sorry. Catch up with you."

I open the door. Pull open the scratched white-flaked screen door. I remember my mother in her shorts and tank top painting it. Over and over she'd paint it. To keep it white. The inner door is stuck. I shove, throw my weight into it and it gives. Specks of splinters fly into the silence. It smells old, empty, like forgotten closet corners. Like the smell of wet cardboard. Dead air. The second thing I notice is the heat. Damp heat. Flat, choking. The carpet is torn, shredded, lined with mouse droppings, smeared with small, neat animal tracks. Old curtains lay limp on the floor. There is an overturned end table, with papers flowing out of one side. I turn to the kitchen. Someone has sprayed white paint over the clay-coloured bricks my father lined on the wall. There are rusted pots on the counter and a shattered dish between the fridge and stove. The kitchen floor seemed chewed through and there are punch marks in the thin fibreboard door of the bathroom. Every inch of care that was created in this house is gone. I can barely breathe under the decay. It seems as though no one has been here for decades.

I remember that my mother wanted hardwood floors. My father came home with a long roll of linoleum designed to look like wood. My mother laid it down, convinced it could pass for the real thing. Her blond curls bent in a corner, cutting the linoleum with a glinty knife, the hot fluorescent bulbs on so late at night.

"What a mess!" Tony breathes beside my ear. "Shit, princess, what happened here?"

He was making matters worse, and the smoke on his breath annoyed me.

"I can't believe it. This is disastrous, huh?" I whisper more to myself.

"Sure is," he agrees.

He kicks at an empty hairspray can. It swooshes beside the discarded drapes and stops with a small "poof!". I run to the rear of the house toward my old bedroom. I stop when I see the wall between my sister's old room and mine ripped completely out. Nail eyes glare at me and shards of wood-teeth grin out from every exposed corner and ridge. It was an impulsive job, left in a state of such isolation and contempt that my eyes fill with tears. Rage, sadness, I don't

know. The wall with the closet gone. We would meas-
ure ourselves there over the years, beside the closet.
The same closet where we'd hide on our parents and
draw lipstick mountains and suns and people until
our fingers would be unwashably red and our mother
would be so upset that she'd blink over and over and
over so fast and we'd laugh while she'd scrub and
laugh while she'd scrub. I wanted that wall now. To
remember, to sit beside and breathe in the red history
marks that ruined my mother's only decent lipstick.

"Holy shit, are you crying?" Tony sputters. "Now,
that's a first." He turns his features more serious, moving toward me. "Hey, no kidding, love, are you alright?"
He tries to hug me, to express concern.

"Go wait outside. Let me be." I shoo him away,
annoyed, furious, sad.

He shuffles out, throwing me a hurt look over his
shoulder, pulling his DKs out of his pocket roughly.

This place is not familiar. Even if the wall is
dented, paint is chipped in the same place where I
threw the baseball in grade eight. Although my sister's
glow-in-the-dark stars still rest on her ceiling and my
mother's tiny plastic lilacs in the small glass jar still sit
on the cupboard top, these small things don't make
sense now. Not in the dust of decay, inside of the
burnt-out voices of my memory. I trudge toward the

window of my parent's room and look into the gnarled wrists and limbs of our forest, and now I hear my daddy's voice:

"If you look hard enough, from this angle, you can see a tiny dot of the river. Look. Look hard. See that blue?" He pointed out, under the pre-winter branches, past the wood-pecked trunks that layered over one another for acres, defending the river.

"Where, where?" We jumped, hands over eyes, straining, straining.

"Right there. There! Like a little fish eye, watching us!" He laughed, his brown eyes crinkling over his wide, sharp cheekbones, his black hair shiny beside the bright window. My Ojibway hero, who I looked nothing like.

"Or a blueberry..." I said, unsure. "Like we pick in the spring."

"Or a blueberry!" he agreed, his laugh as smooth as water, as the soft movements before ceremony.

And then I saw it. A bobbing blueberry balanced between hordes of brown branches. The only colour in the whole backyard. I stared and stared until it blurred away from me, and when I looked again I couldn't find it, no matter how hard I tried. I cried that night, wanting to find it again, that one angle. That one spot.

I see Tony wrestling with a sun-tinged fern, yanking it up roughly and tossing it behind him into the bush. My eyes lift above his head, past a mosquito patch, into the tangle of knobby branches, looking for my daddy's blueberry. Limb upon limb, wood knots, wooded paths snake into each other like a thousand sisters' fingers. And I see it. There. Right there. A small blue fish eye. A glimpse of a bird's wing. My blueberry. And I breathe in home again, laughing. For the relief that familiarity brings. For summer afternoons. For Indian waters behind log houses. For Daddy's big brown hands on daughters' heads. For bird sounds through the windows. For tiny blueberries to drive me home again.

Totem

It was like watching the final erection of a long-carved totem pole come to pass. The slow, careful movements were sentimental, hesitant and, of course, necessary to the journey; that final, ultimate step of completion. It was as though the carvers, the artists, were just finishing the final touches of their lifelong masterpiece. A relaxed cheek whittled here, a solemn lip chiselled there and the eyes overlooking the world in a blankened stare to jut out front. His face finally slid into a death-pose so naturally that I did not doubt its rightness, its necessity, yet for some reason my insides jerked about in harsh, fancy-dance motions that so opposed this calm of his features. I was wrenched into a sick spin that I did not come out of for months. I could not grasp the transformation that I saw on Daddy's face that summer, no matter how I justified it with words, so I just blanked it out before I went mad.

He was not a calm man, even when sleeping. That,

I think, had been my initial revulsion to his death at
first. When my daddy slept, he thrashed about like a
rabbit in a trap, arms flailing bear-like and voice hollering a mountain wind of fury in our little house on
the reserve up in Northern Ontario. My sister and I
would dart up in bed, hugging each other, scared, but
eager to hear the swear words that would froth out of
his curled lips in the night. When his nightmare would
end, we would whisper the bad words to each
other and giggle ourselves back to sleep, secretly
delighted by our newfound knowledge. In the morning, he would come out of his bedroom, his big belly
hanging over his chequered pyjamas, with his elastic
smile that would bend every which way over his wide
cheekbones, his salt and pepper hair wild on his head
like the weeds in our yard.

"Good morning, Daddy!" Billie, the baby, would
shriek and run into his belly, bouncing off of it tram-
poline style. "Sleep well, you big muqwa?"

"Like a bear, my girl!" He would nudge his head at
Mommy, his eyes guffawing at us and whisper, "But
look at your mama, girls, she needs three cups of coffee! Not me. The sun is my caffeine."

Half an hour later, we would stare out of the big living room window, in the same spot where he died slowly
years later, and watch him chop wood until lunchtime,
not stopping for a minute.

Time is a strange doctor. It has healed me into remembrance, cured me into letting Daddy be a movement again and not that wooden, logged Indian that I saw for the longest time, framed into my horizon of thought. I see now the transformation in its phases and not just the end result. I imagine Daddy like a children's picture book, the kind where you flip the pages and the scene changes, until the character has emerged from a beginning point to an end point. However, now, he is all of these things, and not just an end.

Stories. They are what filled our nights. He would not hold back, he would flow like a gushing fountain and we all got drenched, soaked in his worlds. His features would shift fluidly, drifting sand over our minds; a myriad of the senses.

"This scar's from a fight I got into when I lived on the streets!" Daddy would say as he lifted his shirt off a brown shoulder to reveal a long, zigzagging pale white scar.

"Tell us, tell us more about the streets!" we would scream in delight.

Daddy's face turned to a stony, wooden pose. He replied, "The streets are not a fun place, my girls, not a fun place at all..."

My sister and I would hear of hobos and bar-room brawls and drinking under bridges until the moon's shadows made us grow sleepy, and I would fall asleep thinking of my daddy who took us to church every Sunday and what he did before my mom came and saved him.

One day, shortly after Oka, Daddy got sick. He was old suddenly, his jaw skin hanging where it was once stone on brown determined chin. Those eyes that would lift at corners fell into the same defeat as my old dog Smoky's did before Daddy shot him in the backyard as his mouth frothed at us, growling, full of rabies. The car rides stopped, the camping trips, and the jokes slid into mucky corners away from us. He began to stare somewhere into the bushes from his chair in front of the big window in the living room. We all looked and looked but all we saw was green. Sometimes my mom would call his name and he would not move. I wondered where he went at these times. I think of these moments as his first wooden years, but at these times too, beneath the grey hair at his temples, I would see the throbbing of his mind swim. He would be furious under those temples. I would know it, but say nothing.

The first transformation was startling. His friends, used to the fury of his feet, grew weary at the woodenness that crept out to them from the red chair by the window. They remembered him on the front lines at Oka, red band on arm, fighting with his voice, his words, his flesh. Remembered him on the news, fighting for his people, on the band council, the head of the

Peacekeepers Society. His causes. His fight. His people. Remembered his hot tears as he spoke quietly about the residential school. When the men in suits came to get him and his brothers. When nobody stopped them. His eyes would drift off then. His eyes cataracted into whiteness, stared at them frothily until their feet shuffled on our worn carpet. His long, wise replies became short nods or grunts. I noticed though that his mind pulsed steadily underneath this silence. The tube in his throat blocked his words, but not the power of his thoughts or replies. This knowledge scared me and I found myself staring past him into the bushes when we sat together. Maybe he would have preferred my words, but I was young and I felt guiltily healthy.

Years later, on those nights when I would stay over after I'd moved out on my own, the low voice that would echo out of the bedroom croaked through my consciousness like a Halloween wind. I would hear my mother's pattering feet as she rose from the couch automatically to bring in the bedpan. Minutes later, the house shook with coughs louder than the train that would zigzag through the reserve every hour, her thin arms tired from suctioning Daddy's throat, and I'd lay back on the couch. I should have gotten up for her those nights. I could have taken my fear and balled it like a fist for her. I will never forget how her

eyes were weakened those years. She was skeletal in
those death years, a pale-faced shadow that left her
life behind to soothe, comfort and cry at nights alone.
We forgot about Mom as Daddy died. We did not see
her reddened eyes then behind Daddy's death mask.
We ignored the years she spent in the branch-dark-
ened reservation bush as she watched her husband
die. Her feet pitter-pattered on cold floors as she made
fires and gave medicines, enclosed in wooden walls
from the living, and did all this alone.

When he was put in that white room, without his
machines, we knew. We all knew. Those tubes and
whirring, clicking, metallic fiends were the source of
his living and their absence was an exclamation of
ends. The way we all stood together in that room—
finding our own blank piece of wall to float back the
years on—separated us. His breaths held us together,
bonded us into our history of watching the change of
this man, waiting for him to emerge once again as
new. We knew the final minutes, and we gathered
around his closed eyes. He was closed all over, still,
except for the cave of his mouth. I examined the chip
in his front tooth, and sank into his stories, letting his
life drape over me, rage through me, hearing the
sweetgrass breaths of his boyhood, manhood, death-
hood sink into me like a slow dagger. We circled him

into a cradle, fastening his beginning to his end, and I fell, fell into his open mouth, criss-crossing histories with him, living on in them, emptying myself into the contracting of his throat, becoming a quick pulse when his was gone.

Willard

*T*o listen. Let it in. Absorb his light voice. Willard speaks an agony of words. Truth is hard focus. Outside, the wind whips by. We huddle under our tent and listen. Time and location slip away and life becomes a blur of words. Simple language. Voice. He tells us to listen. He tells us to respect. We offer tobacco. He takes it and speaks. I wonder why I could not embrace it before, this lightness of speech. The whispers of my people. The tongues of my ancestors. I ran instead, but now I am back to reclaim it.

His moustache holds light wisps of white, which moves as he speaks. He leans forward, smoking. Blue eyes speak. The wind steals the exhalations, sucks them up away from us, pulls our hair back, whispers its own song behind his teachings. My eyes slide over his cheeks, into the thin lines chiselled there and I think of paths, river ways, of the forces of life that pull at us, tug us forward. Our bodies form an awkward circle, bent into each other, shaping the rotation of life. A spectator sits on a bench several feet down from us, observing thoughtfully, sipping at his Country Style coffee in a detached manner. Our eyes meet and he looks down as though caught. I feel guilty for destroying his entertainment and refocus on the voice of my elder as he shares. Willard shifts his weight on the hard bench and looks at the child in my arms.

"Look at that," he says. "He deserves to have everything."

My baby moves, sensing the attention of new eyes on him, wriggles closer into me, delighted. His warmth against me defies the wind, gives rise to the newness of beginnings, makes me feel important to be given the role of mother. I move my lips over the blond fuzz of his scalp, feel his pulse there and wrap him closer into me. I understand when he speaks of taking things for granted at this minute.

"He could've been born without a spine. Heart problems. Deformed. Think of that." His voice is syrup. Slow. Waiting for the next drip. "You two are fortunate."

I look at my Tony, wanting him to know the seriousness of such statements, the importance of appreciation. He glances at me, the baby, and I cannot tell his thoughts. His eyes travel over me, stopping at my neck. He picks the baby up in his arms and bounces him lightly. His face is a road map of his heart. Too wide open, too obvious. He cannot hide from my eyes. But I cannot tell this time.

My eyes refocus on Willard, the elder from my reserve, sitting on the hard Country Style bench beneath a cool August morning wind, his eyes settling on me, the baby and Tony easily. Matter of fact. Truthfully. With a slow necessity. Here, time is immeasurable. It no longer exists. It becomes something from another lifetime. I lose some senses, but am rewarded with others more necessary. I listen instead of speaking, explaining. With his words comes the smoky hue of tobacco, the damp inhalations of rain that begins to fall overhead, tap-tapping on the canvas above us.

"Ah, rain," he says. "Purification. A good sign."

And then we are silent, the rain guiding our thoughts toward cleansing. River baths. And the long walks we need toward a new understanding. And my son falls asleep under the song of rain. And my feet gather rhythm beneath the waves of rain. And our eyes pull meaning from the offering. And we absorb. And we listen. And the spectator rises in our lack of words and leaves and starts his car and looks at us again and adjusts his mirror and lights a cigarette and drives away. And the rain. And the maps we make with each encounter. And rain.

We leave him and drive the road toward home. We sit together, tracing rain-lines down the windshield.

They look like tears. Or a series of paths, criss-crossed into confusion, landmarked for renewal. For the first time in months I reach out and hold Tony's hand, ready to forgive him. The baby sleeps in the back, and under the grey-tinged sky, life becomes simple again.

My Grandmother's Story

Despite the fact that the surface of the water was slithering with leeches, the bank was filled with small animal tracks and the sun had begun to slide under the crooked line of the horizon, she stepped into the river and walked in until the brown liquid seared her lips. With the palm of her hands, she scrubbed her body, scratched the delicate surface until she felt the sting of the water entering her cuts, and only then did she stop. She opened her mouth slightly, letting rivulets of the murky brownness enter her mouth. It twirled round and round over her tongue, the sides of her cheeks. She swallowed, but the taste of them would not leave her flesh. Looking up, she saw that stars had come out, splattered over the long sky, and she knew that she had to go back soon. She had been gone too long and she would be punished. The squat gray building stood out in the dark, the rows of windows that glowed with yellow lights and she saw the Sisters reading their Bibles, their black heads bowed, their small mouths moving. Joanna knew that they'd seen.

The water clutched at her, wanting to pull her down, but she moved her legs, forced them one at a time to follow each other back onto the bank. She could see her beige panties poking out between the clumps of grass where their bodies had wrestled while a slow ladybug traced a skinny line over the sand. *Ladybug, Ladybug, fly away home, your house is on fire and your children will burn!* She walked to the edge of grass, dug a hole in the damp sand and buried her underwear. The grass was crumpled with body shapes, the sand indented with bum marks, elbow holes, and heel imprints. She knelt down on these prints and let the water drip over them, knowing that the nuns were watching from the window while they pretended to read. She peed on the sand, the hotness dribbling down her leg, the burn between her legs a red agony, which made her crumble. The sand cradled her body, spooned her. She liked the feel of the sand on her cheek, a grainy coldness that soothed her, made her tired. She pressed her body into the earth, inhaled and exhaled slowly and watched the sand pop up and down under her breaths. She closed her eyes for a minute, sighed and stood. Joanna picked up her brown dress, wrapped it around her like a shawl and walked up the embankment, back to the school.

Sister Edna waited inside of the door, her gnarled hand fingering her rosary beads with disdain.

"You're late, Joanna. Were you out carousing with those boys who walked you girls home?"

"No, Sister."

The Sister's eyes trailed down Joanna's legs, at the dried blood that stuck to her legs like tree gum. "You're filthy. Always running in the bush! You know we don't approve of that here. Now get to your room and we will deal with this in the morning."

"Yes, Sister."

The nun watched Joanna inch toward her room, shaking her head. The girl kept her eyes down, hating the hawk-nosed old woman, wanting to lunge at her, but knowing she wouldn't. She turned the corner into the long hallway that led to her room. She did not ask to go to the infirmary. It was no use. She entered the dark room that was filled with rows and rows of cots and sleeping girls and fell into hers without dressing into her nightie, without washing. The blanket was rough on her flesh, but she was cold, so she pulled it up over her ears like her mama used to do back home to keep warm in the Northern Ontario winters.

Joanna thought of her mother then, her mind drifting back to the reserve, to the time when she'd felt safe. Mama was a big woman. Her thick folds of skin would hang out of her dress like unflattened dough. When she'd lift an axe to chop the firewood, her huge arms would shake with the impact, and she'd split the wood in two neat halves that she'd toss over her shoulder onto the pile. When she'd chase the chickens, her stomach would lift and fall onto the top of her thighs and make little thudding noises between the sound of her heavy footsteps. There were six kids then and they would yell and holler, cheering her on, condemning the chickens as they ran. God help the chickens when she'd catch one, which she always did sooner or later. Its little eyes would bulge out of its head as she wrapped a meaty hand around a thin neck, and with one hand, one quick turn of the wrist, *crack*! And the chicken would fall limp in her hands. She'd look over her shoulder at the kids, smile in glee and yell, "Light up the fire, kids, supper's on!" Little footsteps would echo over the wood floors as the kids ran to the woodstove and lit it up while Mama got the chicken ready, and soon the smell of boiling meat would fill the big room.

Joanna wished she was back there, to the time before she was taken by the men in suits. She didn't care if the nights were cold, or if she had to take care of all the kids herself, or even if they only ate scones for weeks at a time. It was still safe, wrapped inside of the bush, cocooned between the river and the tracks, nestled with her brothers and sisters and Mama in a warm heap of blankets on the floor.

When they came she was unprepared, lugging buckets of water from the well to the shack. She had her hair tied back with buckskin, her feet bare beneath a blue cotton dress. Her mother had gone to the sanitarium seven weeks ago, sick with tuberculosis. Being the oldest, she was responsible for the younger kids.

"Joanna Cloudybear?"

"Aaniin."

"Do you live at this residence with your brothers Fred, Butch, Kenny, Bud and your sister Francis?"

"Y..yeah."

"Gather your things quickly and come with us. Pack as little as possible."

"What you do mean, what?"

"Your mother is not coming back. You are now wards of the state. If you don't get your things in a hurry, we will take you all as is. You have five minutes. Now hurry."

Joanna dropped the buckets, ran to find her siblings, but no one was in the shack. It was empty and ransacked, chairs kicked over, blankets tossed in heaps on the floor. She knew they had already been taken by the fancy men. With shaky hands she picked up her sister's tiny shoes and began to cry. What to pack, what to do, walk in circles, find things, gather sweaters, hats, bread. Big, white hands folded around her small brown wrist. She was pulled into a shiny black car and was quiet all the way there. Her sister huddled in her lap, her brothers swarmed together in the backseat.

When they arrived at the school, their hair was shaved off and they stood in lines for days. One of these days stole her brothers away. Led away by a priest, their eyes waved to her and her little sister. Goodbye. Brown cheeks huddled together in tight packs, moon eyes watching the big people with their funny tongues, squinty eyes and hands that pulled one out of the line and pushed forward, rough. Big, white hands that pointed, pulled hair. Joanna clutched her sister tightly, looked down at the top of her exposed scalp. Little clumpy tufts poked through here and there. It was scary how white her scalp was compared to her dark forehead skin. Joanna felt a lump grow in her throat and she swallowed and swallowed, but it wouldn't go away. She ran her hand over her own head, the small rigid, pokey points of remaining hair and stared at a brown smear on the far white wall until it blurred.

She and her sister waited and waited, and soon they were issued a number and shown to their room. White-walled, rows of cots where folded clothes lay, thin-soled shoes placed beneath. No pictures, dream catchers, warm fur rugs. She prayed that her mother was still alive and would come and get them, but it never happened. Life became a series of porridge, lines and learning the new way. She learned to jump at loud voices, wait for footsteps, bite her tongue, pray. She began to think that her old world was a dream, and to forget how her land smelled, her food, her animals. She could not remember her mama's voice after long, or the sound of the train that used to come at night. Years became deep holes where the pieces of her beginnings were buried, and time became tiny wall scratches lined like soldiers beside her bed.

The older girls were allowed to go to dances at the boys' school. The nuns would line them up, count heads and usher them down the stairs, out the door, and into the sharp night.

"No talking, girls! Quiet all the way, or else!" Sister Alice barked, holding up her brown ruler as a warning.

The nuns led the way down the trail toward the boys' school half a mile away. Once inside, the girls were counted and thrust into a blue auditorium, where a record player squeaked away furiously in a corner. The boys would elbow each other and point to Audrey Morningstar who was dancing alone on the floor, eyeing up the best looking boys. Soon, she was circled and the rest of the girls rolled their eyes to each other. By the end of the night most of the girls found a boy to dance with and those who didn't sat in a corner nibbling on the hard little edges of leftover bannock. The nuns talked amongst themselves, occasionally thrusting their rulers between a couple who began dancing too closely, or smacking a boy's hand that fell too low on a girl's backside. They would whisper loudly, pursing their lips.

"Indecent!"

"Must be in their blood, do you suppose?"

"Wild!"

"Uncontrollable!"

One night, at the end-of-season dance, old Sister Agnes had a fall. She was coming down the stairs, tripped and fell headfirst onto the hardwood floors, landing with a wet thud. Black robes flew, feet scurried, small red mouths gasped. Sister Esther called for a doctor while the other nuns cried fitfully around the dark form crumpled on the floor. The students stared with interest from the dance floor while the priests tried herding them out the door to the field. Father Gregorie ordered Father Joseph to escort the boys back up to their rooms, and he and some of the older boys would bring the girls back early. The girls lined up and followed Father Gregorie out the door. Halfway home, Joanna realized that she had forgotten her sweater, and the Father let her go back to get it, as long as she hurried. She ran through the dark trail, her feet hitting the dry dirt with an even rhythm. It reminded her of the drums that her people used to play at powwows. She smiled at the memory, thinking about the hot corn soup and moose stew her family would eat sitting on the dirt or on wood stumps, watching the colourful dancers. She heard the water lapping at the shore down the hill and she ran faster, wanting to get home before it got dark. A figure appeared in front of her and she collided with it, her teeth chattering against each other loudly. She fell onto the ground with a crack, her tailbone hitting a stone or a branch. Tears sprung to her eyes and she rolled onto her stomach, clutching at her lower back.

"Are you alright?"

Joanna looked. It was Father Joseph, leaning over her, concern in his eyes. "Let me help you up." He lifted her to her feet and looked into her eyes. "Are you hurt, little girl?"

Joanna bared her teeth in pain. "Let me down. It hurt."

The Father lowered her back down to the grass and kneeled beside her. "Rest for a minute, then. What are you doing out here at this hour? Why aren't you back in your room?"

Joanna lay back on the cool grass, the pain slowly

subsiding. She opened her eyes to see Father Joseph looming directly above her face. She jumped back, surprised by his closeness. She felt tiny rocks pressing into her back, smelled the familiar scent of earth around her. The sky was darkening and the water had begun to lap more quickly at the shore. Joanna felt goosebumps pop up on her arms. She turned her head and looked up toward the girls' school. The lights were on and she saw several Sisters moving around inside. She wished she were there now and had not gone back to get her sweater.

The Father moved closer and Joanna felt his hand pressing her down harder into the dirt. His breath smelled like vinegar, his neck skin like tobacco. He moved quickly. Hands covered her, pinched, tore, bore down on her like a black bear, breath heavy, nostrils flaring. What had she done? What had she done? The ache in her back was gone, now moved inside of her, filling her, tore out her stomach, ate into her hips, her legs. The back of her skull pounded into the ground, her ears hurt, yellow formed under her eyelids. Joanna tried to breathe deeper, but she couldn't. The weight of the priest sank into her chest.

Footsteps and more voices. She whipped her head around to see more faces, more eyes, more mouths, smiling, smiling. Father Ribald, Father Peters and two older boys were coming up the trail, watching, big-eyed. Where did they come from? They must have stayed later to clean up the dance hall and were just now returning home. Father Joseph's body was lifted. Someone was saving her. Who? There were hushed whispers, some nervous laughter. And then she was turned around, dragged off of the trail, down to the shore, into the sand. She heard roaring in her ears, laughing, breathing, grunting. Voices came from far away. She had sand in her face, pieces of grass in her eyes, the rusty taste of blood on her tongue. She saw flashes of Father Ribald, Father Peters, the two boys who all the girls were admiring earlier, hovering above her.

Joanna fell into silence and stopped moving. Soon, they peeled themselves off of her body, and she still felt hot, burned, even with the cold air lapping at her flesh. She stayed stomach down on the warmed sand and saw a ladybug trailing through the sand, red-backed, beautifully small. She remembered an old story Mama would tell and thought of her mother's brown rough hands, soft and slow. Low whispers began around her, feet appeared, shuffled over the sand. She didn't move, didn't look up at the faces that belonged to the feet, didn't care who. The feet finally walked away, so many of them, and the sand spiralled with their movements, leaving a dusty landscape, blurred and brown. The ladybug slowly travelled until it disappeared over a sand bump, and all that was left was a thin, dark trail. She thought it might come back up on the other side of the sand. Joanna waited and waited for the red shell to re-emerge, but it never did.

Two Birds

She was alright then. Three years ago, back on the reserve, before she left her husband, her kids, her home. Walked out at 5 a.m. and never looked back. Her snakeberry lips that never smiled. Not even then. But at least she wasn't alone. At least she still had hope. A glimpse of her was still visible, even through the held-back tears and behind the spit of her voice. I can hear it now. Her old voice. The last time I visited her house on the reserve. The month that she left. I can hear her now. I drift into our last visit, remembering the dull syrup of her words, the way she looked that cold day in December.

"It wasn't an affair. Not really."

I ask her why not, and my sister Billie shrugs, not wanting to explain. I watch her walk through the kitchen, her slippers thud-thudding on the cracked linoleum.

"When are they gonna fix this?" I ask her.

"I keep calling the band office, but they keep putting me off." She shrugs, "Maybe they wondered why the floor got ruined so fast, I dunno."

The kids run through like a train. Four of them, pushing each other, tripping over each other, hollering. My head bubbles slightly and I think about leaving soon. Three boys and a two-year-old girl tougher than all of them. She has her hands full.

"Moooo-ooooom!" one of the boys yells. I'm not sure which, they all look the same. Twins and one a year younger. Smooth, dark Ojibway skin, almond-eyed mischief.

"Don't scream, don't scream and I'll answer you!" Billie yells back.

"He hit me. On the nose. I think it broke."

"It's not broke, now go play a video game in the room. GO!"

The kids run off together. I force a smile, wondering how she does it. Her husband is at school, trying his luck in another course. His fourth go, but at least he tries.

"How's your hubby doing at school?"

"I guess he found out he likes math. He's going to be an engineer."

"Really?"

"Yeah. I wanna be a forest ranger." She looks at me, hesitant.

"Forest ranger?"

"Yeah, work outdoors, you know. It's a two year course at the college."

"Wow."

"Get the hell away from the kids for a few hours a week. Get them in daycare."

"Nice."

I watch her eat her sandwich, drippy egg yolk trailing down her long brown fingers, her eyes northward out the window staring into the snow-covered brush outside. Billie is still beautiful underneath her black roots, tape-tied glasses, adult acne, dirty housecoat. Somewhere, she still exists.

"It wasn't an affair because he already gave up on us."

"What?"

"It's true. He's never here. What the hell does he expect? The kids don't even like him."

She still looks outside, her thumb rubbing the yolk into her palm. I look around and don't see enough to fill the spaces: a couch, TV on crates, plastic dining room table chipped raw. Kids footprints on the side of the wall. How did they get up there? No pictures, no love, no signs of a yesterday. I see a cross on the other

side of the room, tacked up against the wall, Jesus'
head hanging to the side, eyes looking upward—the
only trace of colour on the wall, besides the crayons,
finger marks and lines of food beside the stove.

"Do you love him?"

"Who?" She looks at me confused.

"The new guy. Who is he? Not Elmer's son, is it?
The young one? God, he's built, but he's too young!"

"No, you don't know him."

"Not Todd, huh?"

"Naw…"

She stands up and throws her sandwich in the
garbage, plate and all. She told me once that she hated
dishes and I figure that this is a protest against it. The
wind blows against the windowpane and she shivers,
pulling her housecoat tighter around her tall, skinny,
droopy body. I wonder if the kids are alright in the
other room. It is very quiet, but I don't want to upset
her any more than she is. I know her well enough to
sense her agitation.

"They put me on Paxil. They figure I'm depressed."

"Well, are you?"

"Holy shit, of course I am. Look at me!"

"Are they working?"

"Aw, I didn't take them. I sold them to one of my
buddy's friends. He's gonna pass them off for some-

thing else, or something. I dunno…" She pauses and looks down.

"Oh."

"I'm too paranoid for medications. Prob'ly make me worse. What happened to the good ol' days when the medicine women would make you a batch of something that would make you all better? How lucky they were then."

I watch her pace, her boobs bouncing under her robe. For such an extraordinarily skinny woman her breasts are oddly large. I can see that her legs are unshaven and that there are bruises on the bones under her knees.

"He had a really big cock."

"Who, dammit?"

"You don't know him, he's from a reserve up north."

"What's his name?"

"You should've seen the look on his face when milk started squirting from my boobs." She laughed, her face crinkling oddly.

"What, you're kidding, right?"

"No, really. She won't give up. Two years old and still hanging from her mama's titties."

"It actually squirted. On him?"

"All over his face. I think he liked it. Who knows?"

"Ugh. Stop. Please."

We both laugh and she plops down on the floor with a weak thud. "It was great. I was so drunk that it's all fuzzy, but I was so sore the next day that I could barely walk. My idiot husband came home from school and didn't even notice. I limped by him, praying that he would. God, I didn't even shower. I wanted him to notice, but of course not."

I watch her pick at her fingers, disappointed. Not knowing what else to say, I stay quiet. She notices me watching and jumps up, quickly.

"I'm gonna make some cocoa. Want some?"

"Naw, I've got to go. Mom wants to take me shopping in town before Wal-Mart closes. I'll come by in a couple of days."

"I'm meeting him again tonight."

"Yeah? You sure this is what you want?"

"No, of course I'm not sure. But I'm sure not living it. Why shouldn't I have some time for myself at nights? Mom doesn't mind watching the kids. I'm back before they get up in the mornings."

"Have fun. See you later, sis."

"Take your time. You're not missing anything."

I walk outside into the Northern air, my flesh hardening. I look back and see her watching me out of the window. I wave and blow her a kiss goodbye, but she doesn't respond. I sigh, but don't look away from her until I realize that her eyes are looking past me, stuck on the white landscape, the coldness, the frost, the two birds huddled together in her tall birch out back.

That First Night

"Where does, you know, love fit into all of this?"

"Love?"

"Yeah, that thing called love."

"Shhh..."

I pull Tony back over me and silence his tongue with my teeth. He is better quiet sometimes. When he speaks with his gut, with his purple thrust, his heat. His hipbone glides over mine. If not for the sweat, we would hear a thud. The sinews. The sweat. If not for the sweat, we would burn.

I met Tony after Christmas. We had to sneak then, to hide from Peter, the others. Tony at my window. Tap. Tap. Taptaptaptaptaptap...I wait. We ate real Italian pizza on my bed after midnight while the baby slept in the next room. Cheese on my chin, where he licks it off. His tongue, always his tongue. Italian pizza and red wine, until I giggle.

"I don't drink much. It only takes one glass for me."

"Until what?" He asks. He always asks.

"Until I feel it."

Tony watches me eat the whole pizza, artichoke fingers in my mouth, my hair. Wine-red lips licking me clean. That first night. On my bed, still hot from the pizza box, still wet from wine drizzles. I let his fingers pull open my shirt. His fingers still not licked clean. I am not so hungry as him. I feel his fast heat against my leg while he slides over my skin. I shake. I see from his smile that he can see my breasts quiver. He stares, quiet, before his tongue is on my collarbone. Sucking my flesh bones, chewing. I rise hot and cold, feel eaten alive. His tongue down between my breasts, through the line of my belly, teeth on my thigh. So fast. I am choked by his speed, made silent by his want.

My ceiling is filled with prickles. Little dots of stucco. So many, like stars. Tony pushes me down and I try to count them fast. My hands in his hair. Pushing him downward, hard. My fingers wrapping his hair in my fist. He grabs the sides of my thighs. Pushes me too far apart. Hurts beautifully. I feel spliced, hammered apart, stretched. His watching delights me to thrust back at him. I like that he doesn't tease. His tongue so fast. The speed. I imagine a woodpecker, jackhammer, little holes in trees. My blankets wine-splattered, look blood-drenched. In my ears. The rush of blood. The rush of fire. I lift, lift, somehow seeming stronger than Tony, overturning his efforts, bubbling. Like a new, strong soup. Corn soup, how it all floats to the top, little baubles of field flesh. I am rising. Bubbling up and now he is the one overcome.

Afterwards, bruised, suckled dry, he nibbles on my pizza crusts, hungry. His eyes are softer, less alert, more refined. He seems older in his languid pose. Looser, less threatening. I watch him, sipping the bottom of my wine, trailing his body with my eyes. So long. So cat-like. Stealthily made. Somehow I know this will last, these midnight trysts, slow sips of wine, hot spots left from pizza boxes, limp questions on pillow tops, closing of windows, goodbyes.

Once, One Summer

Once. I became hypnotized by sweetgrass. One summer. The first time I saw him. Years back, almost
out of the reach of my memory. Nights filled with drumbeats, I danced, lost in the shadows of my youth, filled
with the blood of my grandmothers. I saw him first
beside the glow of a fire, half shadowed, half possessed
by the hot orange light heat. I was reminded of a picture
that I once saw in a magazine showing a beautiful
Cherokee woman. He looked like her, black hair covering him like a shawl, beaded neck and cheekbones jut-
ted, sharp. Eyes slanted like a fierce coyote, not
watching me on purpose. I moved toward him, mobi-
lized by the pulsing powwow rhythms behind me, made
brave by the motions of his fingers on his bronzed lap.
His eyes turned towards me.

"What's up, White girl?"

"White girl?"

"That's right." Slow smile, fox-like, calm.

"Don't you know an Ojibway diva when you see one?" I smiled.

"Whatever, White girl." He walked away, smirking.

I didn't see him again until the next night. Full moon, and the fancy dancers weaved through my vision. Yellow, orange, blue-feathered dreams, etched bright against the dark. Legs lifted up, down, round and round. I leaned back against a tree, sighed and swam in the colours, sated.

"White girls don't know how to dance, or what?"

There he was, his teeth glinty white against his dark sleek skin, perfectly even, pearly. His hair was pulled back in a braid, his brown flesh covered in white buckskin and beads. Inky tattoos out of place on his arms. He was a beautiful Indian man against the moonlight, against the summer-drenched trees.

"I guess not," I replied.

A long, raven-haired woman appeared from the moonlight, draped in black beadwork, leg-length moccasins and edgy, sharp cheekbones winking at me.

"Peter," she said, grabbing his arm, flipping her hair over a shoulder. "Let's go."

She pulled him back under the trees until all I could see was the outline of buckskin beside the green bushes. I turned and stepped toward the music, the fire flames and let the warm summer wind bring me upward.

Later. Drinking water and chewing on long blades of grass, behind the action of the evening, alone, secluded. I watched intently as he and the woman sat down several yards ahead of me while she stroked his braid with her long, earthy fingers. I knew he had seen me.

He looked back and saw that I was watching. Smirk. Slow shift back, chest out. The woman leaned in, the tight leather stretched like elastic over the heavy shape of her breasts, pressed against him possessively. Her tongue darted out, snaky, electric, dipping into his ear, travelling around the depth like a gently moving canoe, languid, slow. His left hand reached up to her breast and roughly squeezed hard until she yelped and pulled back. He grabbed her wrist, twisted it down, and I could see his tongue open her mouth firmly and thrust its way inside. She leaned back, breathless, her chest moving up and down, fast, her brown cheeks pink. He looked over her shoulder to make sure I'd seen. I couldn't look away, didn't want to.

She said something in his ear. He shook his head no, his braid shifting over his shoulder while his slow hand lifted her dress and his long fingers trailed her leg. She let him that night in the dark, as everyone gathered around the dancers and only us here beneath the moon. Her dress was lifted higher, roughly. Caramel thighs quivering. His tongue tipped out beneath his teeth. He seemed malicious, dangerous here outside with no one else around. Her head tilted back, exposing a triumphant, long neck. Her hair draped down her back, currents of black silk. His hands pushed her thighs apart. She was silent, deer-like, proud. Their breaths didn't exist beside the drumbeats, the faraway dancers, the wind-rustles buried in the trees. His jade eyes connected with mine. Not even as he mounted her, not even as she took him in easily, not even as his chest pressed hers in with a thud, thud, thud, thud did she see me as I sat leaning against the tree, silent, except for my breathing, the shallow core of my throat bobbing silently under the black sky, moon traces of brightness on my eyes, my hungry hands digging hard into the quiet dirt.

Peter's Summers

Numb the world flew by the "Welcome to Sault Ste Marie" sign and I was heading once again far from home away from the pine trees and shallow-necked bird songs and I laid my head back happy that I wasn't driving and the world whipped by so fast that I felt dizzy in my stomach when I thought of you and your oak-coloured hands over mine and how you pressed down on me so hard inside of the house that your daddy built years ago not far from the house that my daddy built years ago and where I watched you drum your life-songs into the heart of my senses those summers before when we did it the first time and then it was summer again and your hands were on my throat telling me that you loved the feel of a woman's light throat under your lips and that you love the feel of Ojibway skin in your teeth and that you love hard

Ojibway lust on your skin and I smiled at your words under you and you were so heavy on me that I thought that I would crush under you so heavy on me under you so light so small except the wet need for more for deeper for straight Ojibway love-words in my ear for straight bear claw need down your back for the deliverance of morning for the dewdrops of morning under our feet as we ran to the river naked my breasts bouncing toward our Indian river your eyes tracing my white-girl's ass that I must have inherited from my mother you said when you licked your tongue down it those summers so heated when we skinny-dipped like it was midnight and swam like two otters toward each other's under-river kisses not afraid of bloodsuckers for the first time when I was with you and your blue-water hard flesh that I took in my mouth underwater like a river snake where I swallowed you like a piece of salt pork and full bellied ran toward noontime where you sucked the river water from my body where you pulled the seagrass from my toe creases where we shared the last Bud Light droopy-eyed thrusts where we lay weakly sated where we heard the blare of my sister's horn outside the house that your daddy built years ago not far from the house that my daddy built years ago where I knew I had to go far from home where I left that summer with your baby inside of me where we made such beautiful beginnings where we loved each other where we first started where we thought that we would last forever.

Peter, At Dawn

*T*he door clicks softly behind you, leaving me here to remember you, our evening, our beginnings. My bed is wrinkled, damp with our sweat and the sage of your body left for me to breathe in. You leave me thinking about you. Today there is only the small hint of morning, lush sounds of autumn and the hot imprint of your hands on my flesh.

Dawn when you leave. My body numb, a casual detachment that I can't reach. You want to live here, but I make you leave. At dawn, under the lampshade trees of my street, you turn. Slow, and light a cigarette. My curtains are good for peeking. Heavy acorn cotton. An eye hole. You have welts on your back. Unseen under your leather coat. I would prefer buckskin. If not just for the smell, or the brush on my cheek. Mostly the smell. You are rough like buckskin. Hard as late autumn earth. As deep as sweetgrass fields. I tried to hurt you. Tear your skin. The more I want you the more I want to bite into you. Through the shell of a hazelnut. I have strong teeth. We used to try to crack hazelnuts on our reserve roof. I got through. Hard. Your shell is harder. Sweat trickles. The wet of your spine-curve. I want it but I slip. I want. Slippery. I am naked still behind the curtain, the small bump of my belly starting to show. Nipples brush. You inhale out-side your car. Outside the dawn of my morning, you smoke. Smoke circles, rising. Bathing you, renewing. You don't seem tired under the air-dew, behind your smoke signs. I almost call you back, but you disappear, the exhaust smoke thick in the air. I sit back, sighing. Dawn when I sleep, when I fall back to you.

Remnants Revisited

*D*ead yard. I stand with my little boy on my hip, beside my loom of boxes that I piled up. His eyes are fixed on his sandbox littered with animal tracks and plastic chairs strewn on the ground from last week's brutal winds. We used to play there before his daddy left. Used the grass as an earthy bed. Ate grapes and crabapples. Caught pears falling from the trees. He would throw balls at the cats for Peter and me. Little arms blurry beneath the green, green trees. We killed it so fast. Like always. His daddy left his tools in the garage. I left them there when I packed my things, putting all of his things outside for the world to see. I will leave this place and never look back. The moving truck pulls in and I stay glued, not wanting to leave yet. Not wanting to stay.

I drift inside of our story. Don't say I did it again because I didn't. We can scream and claw and remind each other of bad dreams that we had and you can tell me you love me and I will hate you and we will worry if the neighbours heard and if we woke the baby and you will run out while I fix the door you kicked down and while I try to tape our family picture back together convincing myself that you are a good person and you will go and get stoned somewhere downtown while I nibble on cold chicken and sing our little boy songs with a deadpan voice making plans to run away to some small town where nobody knows us where we can start over and forget you and then you come back and we pretend that nothing happened we fuck and go to bed and press and press replay replay and press replay.

I walk back inside one last time, my son looking for his toys, beginning to whimper, to ask for his daddy. The rooms have been hollowed out. They seem huge, void of ghosts. The air smells empty without our things. I walk to the huge living room window that overlooks the yard. This window. Filled with nose prints. From my baby's fingers. From pink kitten tongues. Remnants of Peter's finger-touches. I run my own finger over them and it smears away. Why is it so easy to clean? To see clear through to the barren yard? Like a lost photo. Full of ants and hungry rats. Fat birds perched on yellowed plants. Suspicious cats peek in from the alley but they don't come in. The garage looms large and vacant but for the mechanics' tools abandoned for the next tenant to find, to use. I take a deep breath and leave this life behind, worried about the life I'll find, the lonely nights, the questions that I see in my son's eyes. I tell the moving men to take it away and click the door closed behind me.

Cedar Fingers

1.

Somehow it all led to this. A walkway of white chrys-
anthemums, soft hands pressing into my arms as I
pass and a violin playing from somewhere far, far
away. Hordes of people smile at me, my white shoes
tapping across the hardwood of a church I barely
know and my future husband stands supported by his
brothers in front of a veil of white lace trim thrown
across a stern, wood pulpit. I cannot possibly know
him. Tony's face seems unfamiliar, his eyes shine with
barely suppressed emotion and his teeth seemed
oddly white under dark, quivering lips. There is the
taste of bile in my mouth. I can feel the quiver of fear
twitching under my eyelids, hear the blood pound
somewhere behind my ears. Feeling very confused
about where I am and how I met this man, I spring
forward in a series of what I feel are small, convulsive

jerks. My sister smiles at me, and I wonder why. I feel on the spot, amplified to unearthly proportions, outrageously stuffed into my crème vintage wedding gown. I am mesmerized by my own irrationality, and I smile, not knowing what else to do.

I didn't really want to get married today. I don't know why I said yes when he asked me in front of my church, his green eyes that he claims are blue shimmering with love, so hopeful, so false. I had looked at the pastor, felt his approval, felt the eyes of his wife on me. The ladies of the church began weeping in unison, nodding slowly, so happy for me, so utterly sincere. The men nodded at each other, remembering their own proposals, their own agitations. I felt a flash of anger at Tony for making such a scene and I hoped that it didn't show in my face. He was so good to my kids, so helpful. He cooked, he cleaned, he made all my friends laugh when he did the chicken dance at a church wedding. I felt cruel for hating him just then. And so I said yes, my eye twitching. And the weeping increased and he disappeared somewhere inside of a circle of men's arms slapping at his back. The ladies swarmed me and I couldn't breathe. They were pulling at my hand to look at the ring that I didn't even realize he had slipped on my finger. My face pressed into perfumed shoulders and a set of pearls indented into my eye, making me see dull, yellow spots.

Three months ago, we moved back to my reserve from Chicago. Packed up what we could, sold the rest, hopped in the van and left. Just like that. We found an interesting walk-up on the third floor and filled it with flowers and new suede furniture and cracked ceramic lamps. We acquired a new life so quickly that it seemed that our old life had never happened. He loved the reserve, thrived here.

"I want to become an Indian, like you, babe. What do I gotta do, huh?"

He was Italian, obviously so, and his accent was so strong that people wondered how long he'd been in the country. I sighed and made a call to find out where and when the sweat lodges were. I dropped him off in the bush on a Wednesday night and waved at him as he stood among a big group of Ojibway, the pink towel that I placed around his neck the only colour that I could see out of my rear-view mirror as I left him there. When I came back, his face was smudged with black soot, and he murmured tribal songs all the way home. It did not intimidate him as I had hoped it would. In fact, he made so many friends on my reserve over the next couple of months that people I had never met began to ask me if I was Antonio's girl, and where he was.

"It was beautiful," he told me. "I've never been to any place like it."

"Where, the healing lodge, or the sweat?"

"The sweat. I mean the healing lodge is beautiful to look at, but the sweat, the sweat was different. Beautiful for the heart. The mind."

I laughed at him, thinking he was joking. "And what do you know about mind or heart beauty?"

He looked down, hurt. "I learned something in there. I'm not kidding. I just can't describe it, that's all." He paused. "Babe, why don't you go? You come from this reserve, you're Ojibway. I mean, this is your culture, why the hell don't you go? I mean, it's right at your fingertips."

"Who are you to lecture me?"

"I...I'm not. I'm just curious. I mean. You wouldn't believe the things that I felt. The way that they accepted me into their circle. The songs, the warmth, the feeling of being set free."

"What are you saying, that I need to be set free? Do you think that something is wrong with me? Come on, Tony, you went *once*! As if you're the big expert."

He didn't say anything else, just tapped on his shoe with a fingernail and watched me quietly. Deep down I knew he was right and this made me angry with him for seeing too much of me, for saying the right thing. For knowing me.

When I took him to my church, he was impressed with the warmth of the congregation. He wooed the ladies until they loved him and they began to tell me how I've hit gold, how lucky I was. I nodded, not knowing how to explain my past to these women, the horrible things we have done to each other, the scenes, the tears. Instead we smile, nodding, curling into each other like those in love. His hand on my back felt hot, like a branding iron, and I took it, knowing how I needed his help, knowing how he knows this. But I must have loved him because I became fiercely protective of him during my family's verbal assaults, during my poor mother's sadness.

"Do you love him? Are you happy?" A breath, with hope that I would shake my head and fall into her arms.

"Mama, please. This is my choice. For now, it is my choice."

A long sigh, a windy pause. "Whatever makes you happy."

2.

Love. I felt it sometimes with him. Little bursts of something close to joy. 3 a.m. one morning and his hands slid underneath the silk of my panties, outlining my flesh-lines with the tips of his fingers. His face was shadowed behind the wisps of night and his arms seemed like tarnished copper beside my face. Between dreams and mornings he could be enough for me. His words were always beautiful, because of the fierceness of his language, the force of his culture. His gentleness during the day was offensive to me, but at night, at night it made him a statue. Flowed him into me in small currents, without force, but with a subtle touch that opened me to him, allowed him to become noble to me, perfect. Our breaths loved each other, were so in synch that my body responded to the rhythm, felt so natural that I rose to meet him, pushed my hips into his, flung my arms around him, his tears dripping down my forehead, into my eye creases, the shadows of my ears.

"You do love me, you do, you do, you do, you do..." Tony whispered.

Other times, my heart would lurch toward him, wanting to pull him into me, to lull his need, to satiate his want. Those times, rocking my newborn to sleep, meows and gurgles and Italian lullabies and little snores of satisfaction. Those times, with the children sick. His concerns, his worried heart, the fevered nights where he could not sleep. Sometimes I would really want him. Want to see the surprise in his face. Want to fill him with more love for me. Want him to never focus elsewhere. Want him to feel something from me close to love. Especially when he left. Furious, I would drag him back to me, and scold him for his escape. Run his bath that evening, lick his wounds, surround our bodies with candles and whisper things to him that did not make sense to me.

Love. I can remember other hands. Bristles of desire, dark hearts, blackened noonday rooms. Pulls of impermanence, the thrill of desperate decadence. I wanted this for a time. Another language meant for love, another's lips, harder touch, a more soothing restlessness. Small escapes outside of motherhood. Tiny excursions into a foreign discomfort, lacking the control I sought. But time and time again, we returned to each other. Missed some sort of medial comfort, lessened for the lack of fire, the lack of fury, a lack of impulse. But I fell in love with him, at times. When he slept, his expressions non-existent, he seemed to me timeless. Lips full and unmoving, hands folded over his chest, the curve of his nostril showing no signs of life. When he first wakes and does not see me yet. The soft movements before the stretch of dawn. The silence of his wakening was impressive, the utter slowness of it. Tony was like a story during these times, like the things you'd find in myths. Like I heard my grandmother say to my father once when we were supposed to be asleep as he cried to her in our kitchen about the residential school that he went to, and she told him about the residential school that she had been to. Through their tears, her endless silences, his own outbursts, his unquenched rage, her calm, she told him: *In silence and peace would vision come to him who was prepared.* Tony made me think of this, reminded me of this. I loved him those times when he got lost to this world, engrossed. That far-off listlessness inside of him that he always controlled. His pure ability for peace. I loved those looks, the ones he never gave me.

3.

He left me once. One September, tired of me slipping back to my ex-boyfriend, Peter.

"I can't take it," Tony told me. "Knowing he is there with you."

"I have to try. We have a baby together. One on the way."

"I love you. I'm leaving town. I can't take it anymore."

"You won't go."

"I have to."

"Go then. For fuck's sake, go then. For once, just do as you say!"

Tony left on the morning train, before I woke. The phone rang and I did not answer, knowing it was him. It rained. The leaves had not changed colour yet. I lay in bed for an hour, my son sleeping. Later that day Peter dropped by, made himself at home and sprawled on the bed. I watched as his hand lay upward on my white duvet cover, yellow cigarette stains lining the insides of his fingers, the colour of old corn. The father of my son, now back, wanting back into my life. He said he would change his last name to mine if I would marry him. He promised to give up cigarettes, beer, the dope. I never believed him, even under the flickering candlelight when he tried to cook for me and burnt dinner and left me with a mess to clean and fell asleep after drinking all the wine and left a bag of weed on the table where my son could have grabbed it. Peter puked all over the bathroom that night and slept all day again and slept all day again and slept all day again. I never believed him because it never began to happen. I wanted him to leave.

When Tony left I was lost. Stuck with this beautiful-framed man who fathered my child who watched me with twitchy jade eyes, leaving me empty, nauseous and afraid for my future.

"Get back here!" I screamed when Tony called. "I can't take it here!"

"But you threw me out and took him in!"

"Don't you understand? We have a baby together. One on the way! I'm two months pregnant!"

"It's not mine. Sometimes I think life would be easier if I just stayed here."

"Get back here!"

"Dump Peter, and you come to me for once."

Two days later, watching Peter sleep through noon, watching his cheeks indent in and out and in and out and in and out, I packed my bags and left with my son. The train to Chicago was beautiful and Tony met me at the station, twirling me and twirling me and we skipped down Lake Street, chewing on french fries and singing windy kids songs about a tigger and bear and no cares and no cares.

4.

I am used to someone screaming back. Seven months pregnant, crazy with rage. The garbage can whizzed by Tony's head, missed and dented the wall. He ducked, trying to reach around my fists, trying to grab my wrists.

"Calm down, you need to calm down, honey."

"You don't love me! I should never have come to Chicago! You stare at every other woman because you think I'm fat!"

"What other women? You're not fat, you have a beautiful baby in there."

"It's not yours, so what the fuck do you care?"

"I do care. I love you. I love him."

"What if it's a girl? What then, huh?"

"Then I love her. Come on, breathe. Breathe."

I grabbed the toaster and threw it, knowing I'm crazy, knowing he's innocent, glad my son was at day-care, glad the neighbours were at work. I tried to bite his shoulder, pull his hair, but he wrapped me in a hug and I bucked to get loose, felt the baby inside of me kicking with passion, kicking at me, lunging at the walls of my belly. This slowed me and I crumpled at his feet, crying, weeping with rage.

"Why don't you just yell back? It would make it easier on me. It really fucking would, you know."

"Don't be silly, I love you."

"You just want me to look like the crazy one and you the good guy, right?"

"No, no. I just want to see your smile."

"I would rather you hit me than play these games."

"Don't be ridiculous."

"Fuck you."

I wanted to hurt him, but at the same time I wanted to stop and let him hug me. *I'm sorry, it's not you, I feel fat, like a hideous beast, thank you for cooking for me and pouring me baths and putting up with my complaining and being so good to my son because his daddy is gone to the streets and thank you for stand- ing by the stove smiling at me while the tea brews and not hitting me back and not yelling back and making this rage end so quickly and so easy.*

I thought of my mother and father. His rages, her ability to calm. Her slippered feet at the stove when my sister and I got scared of Daddy's yelling and hid under the table until he was quiet, until he was asleep.

Tears blurred the world, made all sense turn inward. Saw Tony's feet at the stove, the little hole- mark with the toe tip poking out, saw the curve of his calf, the hairs curling downward toward the brown scuffed rug hiding the blue, diamond, cold linoleum. It was winter and snow was beginning to pile outside of our patio door. The heat in the kitchen stopped working and the landlords were in Florida and did not leave their forwarding address and would be back in April and it was cold and we got lazy, snuggling under blankets, learning how to love each other's closeness because I was too cold to push him away at nights. It began to feel good, my head on his shoulder at night. When I would play with his chest hairs, his breath would still, his body stiff with silence, not wanting to move in case I stopped. I began to kiss his face and suck on his neck skin. Began to warm to the shape of his body, understand why people cuddle and make silly noises inside of each other's caresses. At nights I understood why we needed each other.

His feet walked toward me and I tried to smile, tried to say sorry with my gesture of reaching out and grabbing the tea that he made me. He kneeled and took my hand.

"Your hands are so little, like a child's." He traced the lines softly with a finger.

"They are?"

"Yes. Beautiful. Lovely."

He held my hand as we drank our tea in silence, watching the snow pile up under the sudden dusk that fell.

5.

Back near the reserve, drunk on homemade wine, purple-lipped, I kissed him for the first time, scratching my nails outside of his expensive Italian shirt, wanting to rip it, to impress on him how money does not matter inside of passion. I did not have to because Tony slowly pulled it off, buttons flying under my sister's dresser, resting with her hairclips, earring backings and old cigarette butts.

"You are a princess. What did you say you were again? Russian?" Tony whispered, his Italian accent foggy from the wine.

"Ojibway."

"Is that Polish sort of? Where is that?"

"Indian. North American. Indian. Native Indian."

"But you look European. Russian. Your skin is so fair…"

"Well, a little Swedish, on my mother's side. But mostly Indian."

"Well, you sure are a princess. Come here, come here…"

His hands slid over my back, hesitant on top of my backside. His touch was gentle, and this was annoying me. I pressed my back into him, trying to speed him up, trying to move him into a more aggressive pose, but he was insistent on his purpose. I wondered how long I could stay next door at my sister's and put the sitter off. I bit his sugary neck and he pulled away, cupping my chin. His breath found my ear, singed the tip of it, made little sucking sounds, blocking everything else out. I could no longer hear the sound of my sister's laughter outside of the bedroom door, high and lilting, fake. Could no longer hear the pulsation of music inside of this room. His breath overrode it all, quiet, insistent, slow. And I thought of birds' wings. Flutter of

wings. Butterflies, dragonflies, ladybugs as they drift
away. I thought of the reserve, the slow water in the fall
behind my house, steady drips of syrup from the trees.
Thought of bear prints and rabbit tracks and how they
lined their way into the dense dirt of my land. I lost
myself in this slow arrival, shrugged off the newfound
acceptance as drunken misunderstanding and barely
remembered our first kiss.

6.

A few weeks after we met, Tony had taken an apartment not far from the reserve, in the nearby city. I
woke up to find my back window had been smashed,
blood smeared around the back door entrance in tiny
dribbles. The sectional couch was pulled apart from
the wall, the coffee table was overturned and the vase
on top chipped apart, small egg-coloured pieces
splayed over the carpet. I screamed out the door for
my sister, lifted my son into my arms and ran from
room to room to see what was going on. The kitchen
coffee pot had been smashed on the parquet floor,
jagged edging glinting under the harsh kitchen lights,
beside the buttercup walls. The drawers from the cupboard had all been pulled out and looked like tongues

sticking out, mocking me. Blood dribbles led me to where he must have gone. Furious, I stormed into the back bedroom where I found Tony. He was passed out, drunk, his shirt ripped open to reveal his chest zigzagged with skid marks and red wounds. Blood pressed through the shirt-sleeves, polka-dotting the fabric into further ruin. His mouth hung open, slack, loose and vulnerable. I ran forward to check to see if he was still breathing. He was, and I was pissed off at the condition of my white duvet cover. Splatters of red splashed over the cotton overlay. Blood was seeping straight through, destroying the duvet underneath. I would not ask him to replace it. I couldn't face him right now.

Earlier we went dancing in the city. Salsa at the club. Skirt-twirls, quick steps and tequila breath in my ear. His grip was harder, more aggressive on my back. His eyelids drooped toward me, his lip twisted up, menacingly.

"You wanna dance with him, don't you?"

"What? Who?" I looked behind him, knowing who he was talking about.

"You know who, stop playing stupid."

I laughed and twirled away, dancing alone, my long skirt twirling, my long black hair bouncing against my back, the world a blur behind me. I could

feel Tony's eyes on me, watching me. I noticed a familiar shape leaned against the bar. It was Peter. I sensed
Tony at the bar again, out of the corner of my eye, saw
his hand lift, throw back more shots, resume his
drunken pacing. Peter approached me, forced his
body against mine on the dance floor. Squished
between the sweat, the energy of the music and his
breath on my neck left a fury behind, lacing down my
spine, dizzying me. His shoulders were strong, his
shirt a thin white cotton that brushed against my
cheek. His lips were the colour of faded blackberries
and his jawline was lined with short stubble that
brushed into the flesh of my forehead, making me feel
afraid instead of safe. His face was a shadow beside
my eyes.

Then the hands everywhere. Pulled us apart. The
sound of wet flesh overpowering the music. Red-
tipped fists colliding into each other. The blur of Peter
and Tony reminded me of two bucks locking into each
other, yanking at each other and I ran, fell out the
door before they could see me, into a cab, into my
front door. Sent my sister home, showered and
crawled into bed beside my son, healed by his soft
breaths, his little hands that I curled into my own as
he slept, and for the first time in years, began to pray.

7.

The labour pains came suddenly. Yellowed dishwater covered my hands and I doubled over, my enormous belly crashing into my upper thighs. Searing heat filled my back and I knew the baby was coming. I sat down on the floor heavily, glad that my mother had come from the reserve last week to be in Chicago with me. She had missed the birth of my first son and had come by Greyhound early this time so not to miss this one. The floor was shining, cleaned by Tony yesterday, scrubbed down with an oversized blue scrub brush while I watched. The old brown carpet had been discarded in the process.

"It has to be perfect, please. I can't stand it, this huge mess."

"You've been cleaning for weeks. There's no mess, honey. The apartment is sparkling."

Earlier that week, Tony mopping the floor. "Please Tony, please. Use more solution."

His back curved round in a large hump, shaking with the motions of his intense scrubbing. I sprayed and wiped the microwave while he did this, making sure he didn't miss a spot. My mother came out from the bedroom and laughed at us, telling me that I look like a little bird getting her nest ready.

"Little? Geez mom, have you looked at me lately? I'm a beast."

"You're gorgeous, honey."

"That's what I've been telling her," Tony agreed with my mother.

She rubbed my lower back as we stood in the kitchen, little circles of pressure round and round, blending with the scrubbing on the floor, the little scratch-scratch motions soothing me.

The triangles of the linoleum shone. I lifted my shirt to look at my belly. It gyrated strangely. I was waiting for a new pain, a further revelation of the impending birth. A heat spread through my upper legs, as though my bones were being branded savagely. I watched my baby shift fluidly, elbowing and kneeing into the walls of my belly, stretching and begging for more room. My bellybutton pushed outward, straining, my skin pulling tightly under the bulk of the baby inside of me. A new contraction came slowly, built up to a peak where my breath could not exhale, where my belly seized into a tight, hardened mass of flesh. Sweat broke out behind my neck, my nails grabbed the edge of a cupboard handle, my eyes squeezed tightly closed. I felt hands lift me, did not fight it, did not question their strength. I knew Tony had found me, would take care of me, would not let me suffer alone. He laid me down on my couch and whispered to me over and over.

"Breathe baby, breathe. Breathe, honey. Give me your hand. I am here. I am here."

I never looked at him during this time, just let him touch me. My hair was smoothed back, brows wiped with a warm cloth. Where this would normally annoy me, it was what I needed now, what I wanted. I was afraid, excited, tense, felt like nothing was ready, like I had been ready forever. All at once I felt everything, the sliding away from my youth even further, the loss of my childish bond with my own mother, my eagerness to hold onto the past stretched out of my reach, a wild hope for the future and the intense need to hold what is inside of me and never let go. I wanted this baby's breath on my cheek more than anything in the world, to hear a first cry, to escape from this weight tugging me downward, pulling me to my knees, swollen hands on the floor, tears on the hardwood, cheek on his knee, whispering.

"They're hurting more, coming faster. Let's go now, okay?"

I was hustled out, barely thinking, only feeling, waiting, breathing. To a hospital in a city that was not my own, but his. To a doctor who's face I had never seen. To hands that would tear my baby out of me. I let him lead me, seeing the shape of my three-year-old son sleeping on the pullout couch that I found in the alley the summer before. Saw the orange of his wrinkled Tigger pyjamas, his small face pressed into the sheet, oblivious of my departure, my pain. I remembered my oldest son's first howls, the purple of his face, my startled glimpse of love, not caring who saw me cry, not caring anymore that his father was stoned, not caring that my old life was gone. My big baby, still so small, curled up, my mother watching over him.

"Go," my mother whispered. And I did, the March wind tearing into me, momentarily easing me away from the pain.

8.

I was driving. Drops of rain were brushed away by my wipers, the sound soothing. Tony sat beside me adjusting the radio dial, glancing at me, wanting to talk about our earlier fight, wanting to hear me explain, say that I'm sorry. I turned left at the corner and ignored his loud breaths, his tapping fingers against the door handle.

"Listen," I began, "You knew it wasn't yours all along. You knew."

"But you told me it was."

"It was just easier that way, okay."

"Yes, it was."

"Now let's just go get some ice cream. Let's just relax and forget it, okay?" I almost missed the stop sign at the next corner and the rain made the road slippery.

"Shit, watch it!"

"Well, you're getting me all worked up talking about this. It's not your baby and I won't let it be Peter's. It's just mine, okay. Now shut up about it."

"Peter's an asshole. What did you ever see in him?"

"For God's sake, you don't stop, do you?"

"I'll kill him when I see him."

We drove in silence, the window occasionally smeared, blurring the yellow line in the middle of the road. I flipped on the heat, the rear wiper in the van, and let Tony's breaths calm my own. He unrolled the window and lit a smoke.

"Hey. My son's in the backseat sleeping. No smoking in the van."

" Listen, it's the least you can do. Let me smoke. Just this once. Shit, hon, you're breaking me down."

"Go ahead then. Smoke. Just this once."

The rain flew in. I turned up the heat, watched him poke his chin out the window, puffing urgently. His black eyebrows were wet, slicked flat on his forehead, and rain made tears down his cheeks that flew back to me. I felt a pang of regret that it wasn't his child, that

I could not give him what he wanted. I wondered if I loved him, wondered what it was that kept us together, what kept him accepting me no matter what. He was unshaven, rough for once, his clothes wrinkled. We waited until my son fell asleep to talk again, but now the fire was out. I knew if I opened my mouth that something horrible would erupt. I knew how I hurt him over and over, how my words could not be gentle with him.

"Look," I said, attempting to reconcile. "I wish I could change it, but I can't."

He did not move, just let the rain fly over his face. His cigarette was getting soaked, little dots of wetness over the thin white paper. The tip burned orange. He inhaled, closing his eyes, the rain covering his face as I turned the corner. The cigarette broke in half out the window, his hand still clutched it tight, and he exhaled. Smoke blew back toward him like an offering, making me sad for him choosing to share his life with me when I could not bring myself to work with him, to love him like I loved the others. Closing the window, releasing the butt of the cigarette, he sighed, wet with the afternoon rain.

"It all doesn't matter." He sighed. "I'll work with you through this."

I drove, not responding, my stomach tied in knots over my future, over my past and over this man who sat beside me absorbing my life and patting my hand with his own, damp and cold.

9.

"Leave with me, Tony," I whispered to him at 3 a.m. "Chicago is killing me. I want to go home."

"But your mother was here, and the birth went so smoothly...We have two beautiful children here. We can build something out of this. Why do you want to go, honey?" He sat up, his chest bare, the hairs lined haphazardly over his chest.

"Go back to bed. We're going to wake the kids."

I glanced at my tiny son asleep on his back inside of his crib beside my bed and my three-year-old asleep beside me, arms sprawled outward, relaxed. "Apart from you, there's no reason for me to be here. My family's on the reserve. I want my children to know their culture, their heritage."

"You want to go back to the reserve?" Tony lay back down. "Come on, sugar, let's talk about this tomorrow."

"You'd better decide soon whether or not you want to come. I have to go." I turned my back to him and took my three-year-old into my arms, tight, saying a prayer over and over for God to give me a sign, a dream, something to tell me what to do, where to go, inhaling the smell of my boy's hair, basking in the warmth of his breath.

I lay up for the rest of the night, dreaming of moving away, knowing I had to, hoping that it was the right thing to do. I could not stay here, could not function, could not think, could not bounce between hatred and love. Maybe I could leave here, leave every image of my experiences here, every remembrance, and walk away with Tony where I could really love him. Back home to my family. Distract myself out of this fog that I feel. Escape once and for all.

Tony's snores soothed me in some inconceivable way. The hard shape of his arm over top of my hip was a small comfort for some reason. The puffs of breath on my back skin were warm and made me shiver, huddle down lower under my comforters. I would not be comfortable with anyone else, could not be my real self with anyone but Tony. I don't know what I would have done without him. I snuggled back into the heat of his body and he pulled me close. I wrapped his arm around me and let his heartbeat rock me into comfort. I knew he would leave with me, quit his job, leave his family, friends. And I needed him, wanted him to come with me. I watched my children sleep, kept my eyes on their chests, the rise and fall, the little night movements that children have, the half smiles, the shape of peace on their faces.

10.

We are building a house. The land behind us has taken us in, framed us into their landscape. My home, these Northern woods. My wedding ring glints when I move my arm up and down, pointing at Tony to do this or that. The baby rests heavy on my hip. My almost four-year-old pulls at my shirt. At nights I don't dream. Days, I plan ahead, my mind occupied. I have found a comfortable place that exists between living and dying, ecstasy and hopelessness. A perfect tepidness without the edge of joy, despair. I have found love here, in the land, in the chirping of birds, in the breaking of twigs under my feet. The love that I left I don't think of here—out of self-protection, out of the fear of longing, or the emptiness that want brings. I try not to hear old voices, or to feel old hands on my skin. It is better for me, for my children to have a mother that is grounded away from the past, away from the heat of the unknown. Here, the wind blows warm, nudges my family toward a strong unity, allows us to stand together, firm, watching for eagle feathers, planting gardens, reading scriptures to give sense to this place that has given and taken and given and taken.

There are mountains across the tracks, across the

field, from the house that we are making. We can see
their grey edging through the hulks of the trees, beside
the length of the horizon. In the fall, the oranges, reds,
yellows spread their hues over them like hides strewn
over a teepee. Their tips are not high enough to reach
the clouds. On foggy days they disappear. After rainy
days, small rainbows play around their heads. They
seem to block the place where I came from. I tell my
kids that they were born on the other side of the mountains, that we brought them here, back to Mommy's
birthplace, back to the lands of their people, to learn
and to love and to play here. I had big windows made
to face these mountains, positioned for the view in
mind, the branches of my cedar trees framing them
like a portrait, or like two elders bending over a sleeping child, blessing him. Thin cedar fingers whose
smells waft into me, making me think of the sweat
lodge. How my daddy tried to urge me into one. How
I refused. How he explained to me during his death
years how our people brushed the rocks with cedar
branches. His favourite smell was cedar. For the
aroma, for the meaning inside of the smell. In my new
house I know that I will keep watch to these mountains, in wait. In wait for what, I don't know, but there
is something inside of me telling me to wait, wait. It

will come. It will come. Behind these cedar fingers I will sit, the whispers of my grandmothers urging me toward movement, toward the first brush of a long cedar branch over a hot, smooth rock.